GERTIE POOL

A Historical Novel

CRY FOR FREEDOM

ISBN: 978-1-77069-266-4

Word Alive Press
131 Cordite Road, Winnipeg, MB R3W 1S1
www.wordalivepress.ca

Library and Archives Canada Cataloguing in Publication

Pool, Gertie, 1935-
Cry for freedom / Gertie Pool.

ISBN 978-1-77069-266-4

I. Title.

PS8631.O59C79 2011 C813'.6 C2011-901239-1

DEDICATION

Cry for Freedom is dedicated
to my loving husband, John,
for his cheerful and steady encouragements;
to our children—Gail, Cindy, and John Dwayne—
for lending me their shoulders to lean on for inspiration;
to my loving parents, for exemplifying an unwavering spirit
of faith, hope, and love in trying times;
to all my siblings, scattered around the globe and living in
Holland, Alberta, and British Columbia today.

The purpose of this writing is
to demonstrate my deepest respect
to those who freely gave their lives
so that we could taste the joy of freedom today;
to keep history alive and give
younger generations a chance;
to learn to respect the sacrifices that were made;
and to give our children a far better way of life today.

TABLE OF CONTENTS

LEST WE FORGET

by Gertie Pool

Between the tombstones, row by row
Flowers and red roses grow
Whispering a mystery of love deep
It is here where valour sleeps
Men and youth who gave their all
Who for their country did fall
Their Courage tried on earth, sea, and sky
When a dictator trumpet to mortify
History in gloomy silence tells
How manholes opened up to hell
Speckled in grease-grime and chilling cold
Soldiers showed courage ever so bold
Dauntless in the face of death
Stood tall up to their last breath

1

Invasion

The events that happened on May 10, 1940 turned forty-six-year-old Derk OpdenDries' twelve-member family's life upside-down. The very tapestry of their usually peaceful lifestyle was now torn to shreds. Derk's lifelong dream—gone! Vanished into oblivion. But nothing would deter him from picking up the unravelled threads of his life and trying to mend the tapestry of their family together once more.

Respected town Councillor, CEO of the Dutch Unitas Union, President of the large Anti-Revolutionary Political Party, and manager of three textile manufacturing companies, Derk and his forty-five-year-old wife Gerda lived in stately red-bricked home in the picturesque city of Nyverdal, nestled in the heart of Holland. The family enjoyed living straight across from the always busy and majestic flour-grinding windmill, with its large, clear yard where the neighbourhood children had plenty of room to play games when the mill closed down for business hours at night and on weekends.

Derk and Gerda were God-fearing Christian parents who tried to raise their eight sons and two daughters to become respectable, kind and caring citizens in due time

Gerda was a small motherly woman, slender and elegantly dressed. Her face, round and pretty with lively deep blue button eyes, had an easy smile. Gerda's cheerful temperament enabled her to bounce back from most any difficult situation with a certain kind of humour that helped her raise a close-knit happy family. Heaven only knew how this specific character attribute of hers was to carry them through some of the most difficult challenges that lay ahead of them.

Derk was a man with high moral standards. He had a gentleness in him that showed in his mannerisms. He had a medium build and a well-shaped face with a head of pitch-black hair that curled slightly. His sensitive deep brown eyes saw far deeper than the way things looked on the surface. Derk was born with a keen philosophical attitude in dealing with people.

Derk was known to be one of the toughest union bosses when it came to matters of fairness and justice in the workplace. The union membership admired his strong, fair mentality, which he demonstrated when it counted most.

He was blessed with an organized mind, easy manner in dealing with people, and a quiet self-confidence that demanded attention every time he spoke. His speech was what one would call "very proper and mannered" most all the time.

The two thousand five hundred union members at the textile factory where Derk had been employed for the past thirty-five years knew him as a straightforward, "look-em-in-the-eye" personality, not afraid in the least to handle difficult situations and sneering remarks with ease. He was respected and feared at times for voicing his opinions truthfully, fearlessly, and with total disregard for negative criticism when an unjust action took place anywhere near him.

Early morning on May 10 1940, things went terribly wrong.

Dawn was slowly receding to allow nature's creative splendour to explode into a bright, sunny day. It was scarcely six o'clock. Derk could smell the fresh scents of early spring through the bathroom window, left open through the night, and could hear the chirping birds loudly proclaiming their cheer and happiness as if to awaken a slumbering neighbourhood to come listen to their delightful chorus.

He slipped out of bed. Derk walked over to the window and noticed the first light of dawn touching the roofs of the houses in the neighbourhood. He looked out the window and noticed the horizon gradually lighten with colour in the half-light of the morning light. Derk took a little time to observe creation's unfolding beauty. He stood quietly watching the artistic grandeur of the dwindling sunrise paint soft purple and gold colours in the east, creating a crimson shine over small clusters of clouds settled over the horizon.

It was as if nature was trying to slowly awaken the five thousand residents of this thriving manufacturing town. Most the Nyverdal residents made their living working at one of the three linen factories near the outskirts of the village.

Derk made his way over to the bathroom mirror. He recognized he'd spent too much time day dreaming. He quickly brushed his teeth and combed his wavy, pitch-black hair. He washed and dressed hurriedly in his dark blue suit, white shirt, and matching tie, and left the room. He took a quick look at the clock hanging above the door at the end of the hallway.

I only have fifteen minutes to get to the office for an early morning breakfast meeting with union officials. I best hurry along.

He was to preside over a hastily-called membership gathering at the textile factory. *The same factory I was hired at thirty-three years ago, when I was only twelve years old.* Derk smiled at the thought. He reached down for his suitcase at the end of the hallway and opened the door. He took the utmost care to turn the key very quietly from the outside, so he would not wake the rest of his family so early in the morning.

Derk was known to be an optimistic man in most any circumstance thrown his way. This day, however, his eyes reflected worry. His heart felt heavy as he pushed his bicycle down the cobbled sidewalk that snaked its way through the lush green lawns surrounding his property. He was concerned over the large union membership roll. Deep down inside, he knew just how much the five thousand members were distressed about the constant whispers and rumours of an approaching war and possible invasion of enemy troops. Derk clearly sensed that the membership was terribly worried about job security in case a war with neighbouring Germany were to come true.

Derk came to Main Street. He stepped onto the narrow, sandy pathway running beside the road that led to the factory where his office was. A mild, cool breeze met his freshly groomed face. He pulled up the collar of his jacket snug around his neck.

Suddenly, he heard a low, rumbling noise in the distance. The noises grew louder and louder. Derk stopped. He grabbed the tiny binoculars, which he always kept handy for early morning bird watching, out of his pocket. He scanned the horizon and noticed small specks in the far distance coming towards him. They grew bigger and bigger. Derk felt an uneasy feeling come over him. A strange, unwelcome despair rocked his soul. The dull, steady, unsettling noises grew louder.

Airplanes. Invasion! They are here!

The harsh reality of this looming war rocked his soul like well-placed dynamite. Derk looked around him, but the noise grew louder. Pitch black specks on the horizon loomed larger every second that went by. There seemed to be dozens of airplanes speeding towards him. *War!* The thought kept banging inside his head. He quickly turned around and raced back home. Everything was crashing inward, collapsing. He had to keep Gerda and his family secure at all costs. *Oh, this ruthless enemy invasion of the country I love!*

He fumbled to get the house key out of his coat pocket to open the front door. He looked up into the sky, which had grown dark. The noise was bewildering. Perhaps there were a hundred or more airplanes above him.

Derk heard footsteps racing down the stairs. The door swung open.

"Dad, Dad! They've come! Invasion! I told you, didn't I?" His oldest son, twenty-year-old Josh, was speaking much louder than he usually did.

The sky echoed with anti-aircraft guns targeting low-flying transport planes. Then came the soft, rushing noises of dozens of parachutes releasing. German paratroopers slowly descended above them. Hundreds of soldiers landed on the soft, dewy ground all over Holland. The almost serene rustling noises of the opening parachutes and frightening drumming noises of the airplanes stirred the still-dozing residents of the small country.

"Come on, Dad, hurry! We need to talk!" The handsome, smooth-talking, dark-haired Josh, taller than his dad already, ran ahead of Derk to get to the living room window. He roughly shoved aside the dining room curtains.

Meanwhile, Josh's six brothers and Hennie, his seventeen-year-old sister, came running down the stairs. They all stared out the window.

"What's happening, Dad?" Derk's second oldest, Martin, shouted nervously.

Derk moved to stand beside his seven older children. The three youngest were asleep still. Hennie moved to stand beside Derk. Her usually friendly face had a frown on it. She cast an anxious look up at Derk, then turned her face to look down the street. Hennie's worried eyes fixed an unblinking stare at what she saw before her eyes. Everyone stood in dazed silence, watching soldiers in German uniforms scrambling to pack their parachutes, then make ready their machine guns in case they met Dutch resistance fighters.

More and more groups of enemy soldiers began to form small units in front of the open space by the windmill.

Nuts! All in the name of conquering the whole, wide world for his own. Derk felt agitated. He moved away from the window, walked off a few paces, then returned. His mind was working at blinding speed as he recalled stories his father-in-law, Dan, had told him about the living conditions when he had been a soldier in the First World War. Dan himself had watched young children and older people die literally in front of his own eyes from hunger, cold, and lack of shelter in the winter.

How will Gerda adapt to having to raise our family under the different living conditions that are sure to come? Will there be enough food to feed the family? A cold shiver ran down his spine. *How will this invasion affect all the people I work with in the textile factories in town?*

Questions kept piling up in his mind. A sigh escaped his heavy heart. How would the actions of this nutty, power hungry, and feared German dictator Adolf Hitler affect the lives of his family and the well-being of every citizen in Holland?

Josh made an abrupt turn to face Derk. He had the look of determination. "What are we going to do, Dad? Can't we do something to fight back?"

"Yes, all of us. Let's go set up a plan," echoed Tom, the youngest of these four boys. "Sure, we can figure out something, Dad. Let's sock it to them. Beat them out of our country, now!"

OpdenDries frowned. For some time already, he had recognized that there was a stubborn, fighting spirit in some members of his own family. Some of his boys had begun to prove this fact a few times too many for his liking.

Derk stood silently, pondering just how to phrase his response and instil in his boys the right kind of fear. He himself had learned throughout his life that a little fear could make one cautious, but too much fear could rob one of valuable ambition. Derk sighed.

"Hitler's feared invasion has become reality, boys. We must face this together, as a family," he said calmly. But the narrow slit of his eyes and the firm set of his jaw revealed that Derk himself had already come to a silent decision himself. He turned. "Got to wake Mom and tell her." Derk's heart started beating faster. At the moment, his nerves felt like a bowstring.

Suddenly, the bedroom door swung open wide. Gerda appeared, bewildered, dressed in her nightgown. She directed an anxious glance in Derk's direction, silently trembling with smothered fear.

"Derk, they are here. The Germans! Invasion! What can we do?" Gerda bit her lip. She looked as if she was ready to begin weeping

The usually elegant, calm Gerda clung onto him in fear. Her eyes started swimming in tears. It seemed so wrong that in the midst of the usually early morning tranquility, one lone dictator had the power to invade other countries and cause so much misery, death, and destruction. Gerda's body shivered with fear.

She slumped down on a chair, pondering the dire consequences this brutal invasion would have on the lives of her family and all her loved ones.

"What about our family, Derk? What will happen to them?" She cried softly.

Derk felt a shiver of anxiety run through her. Her body was trembling. He swallowed hard, forcing a smile, but there was no joy in his eyes. "Come, Gerda. Come along, have a look." He took her by the hand and walked towards the living room window where the boys and Hennie were standing already. Derk thrust his chin forward in a defiant gesture. He pointed out the window. "See, there! Gerda, look what's happening." His voice sounded more bitter then he intended it to be. "Oh, that gruesome, selfish dictator!" Derk spoke with deep concern in his voice.

Awestruck, Gerda watched as German soldiers continued to pick up their gear, hustling to take their places in the different groups of army units that had filled the windmill yard.

Heavy silence blanketed the room. Only the steady ticking of the large grandfather clock on the east wall disturbed the unusual quiet inside the house.

Derk turned around and made his way over to the radio on the large oak dresser, a deep frown shadowing his face. He turned on the morning news. The radio announcer boomed out the news nobody wanted to hear: "Early this morning, thousands of German paratroopers invaded our country, gathering in large open spaces and wooded areas," the deep voice of the news reporter announced. "More heavily armed troops forced their way across Dutch borders. The surprise attack met with little resistance from the Dutch army. Holland has been invaded without warning or declaration of war."

Derk walked over to Gerda, his face alight with tenderness. He placed both his hands on her shoulders and tried looking through the tears into her pretty blue eyes. "My always courageous Gerda." He squeezed her hands gently. Derk spoke with renewed assurance. "Together we will weather this storm, as a family. Let's all go pray to our heavenly Father."

Derk moved to stand behind Gerda's chair. He put his hands on her shoulders once more. The firm feel of Derk's hands revived Gerda's courage. The rest of the family huddled around their parents.

"Dear Father up above, You know how much we as a family and all the world needs Your guiding hand in the days to come. Please help to guide and protect each of us from harm or danger. Lord, we know not what will happen come tomorrow, but we truly put all our trust in You, no matter what the future has in store for us in the coming days and years."

That very day—May 10, 1940—Holland became the sixth nation to fall under Hitler's rule, a powerful German dictator gone mad.

Derk and Gerda's long held fears had come to fruition.

2

Orders from the Fuhrer!

The late summer mist playfully turned the dewy grass around their dwelling into a twinkling blanket of early morning wonder. The mist lay shimmering on brightly coloured red and yellow apples on the various trees in the orchard. The inspiring wonder graciously painted the last roses nestled under the freshly filled autumn flower arrangements hanging in baskets near the main entrance of the house.

It was September 1943. Derk OpdenDries grabbed his bike out of the garage, hung his little black suitcase on the handlebar, and walked his bike on the sidewalk under an arch of birch tree branches which still bore a few autumn leaves. At the end of the sidewalk, Derk hopped on the hard rubber-wheeled bicycle. *No sense complaining about the rubber tires. At least I still have a bike. Many people don't.* As he started peddling, Derk lifted his left hand to wave goodbye to Gerda, who was standing inside the house's front window.

On his way to start work at the factory, Derk thought about the German soldiers roaming their streets day and night. He was acutely aware how that the Dutch people had been under the pressures of war for over three years now. The German army just recently had begun to overtake all the schools and large office buildings to live in and set up headquarters around the town.

There seemed no relief in sight. Food was getting scarce and heating fuel was hard to come by. Peddling down the main road, a dark streak of worries inhabited Derk's usually optimistic spirit. *How will Gerda and the family survive throughout the coming winter and the months ahead?*

Rounding the curve at the end of Mill Street, where he lived, he heard loud noises. The situation drew his attention. Derk studied the unusual gathering at this particular hour. He saw a group of flat grey and pie-shaped woollen hats that most people wore to work. They were wildly bobbing up and down. Derk sensed trouble.

He knew most these people from his workplace. He jumped off his bike and placed it against a light pole nearby and hurried over to where most the activities were centered. The rowdy group did not notice him at first.

A tall, broad-shouldered man named Jack turned around and caught sight of Derk. He had friendly, grey-green eyes and a mob of dark brown hair. Jack's roughened hands were big and his face rough, red, and blotchy. He grabbed hold of Derk's shoulders and fixed an unblinking stare at him. Jack roughly shoved the much smaller Derk towards the centre of the crowd. Derk cringed; Jack's fingernails were digging into his shoulders.

Jack's sharp stare bored into Derk's eyes from behind a long, pointed nose. "Here, what do you think about this doggone, lousy Hitler's new orders, big-boss? Look at them! Look at it! That lousy Fuhrer, anyhow!" Jack's voice boomed harsh and gritty. He had a bitter smile on his face.

Jack let go of Derk's shoulders, mercifully. He pointed a crooked index finger towards a large, bright, yellow-painted metal poster hammered onto a wooden light pole.

"Here! See! What you thinking about that, big-boss?" Jack screeched in Derk's right ear. "Tell us, boss, what you thinking?"

Derk did not have to get any closer. Anyone in the circle could see the big, bold letters from far away:

Orders from the Fuhrer!

1. Every male, 18–45 years old:

   Report for work camps in Germany.

   Report at City Hall within two days.

2. Total darkness to be observed evening and night.

Electricity must be shut off from 5:00 p.m.–6 a.m.

3. Resident curfew to be observed from 6:00 p.m.–6 a.m.

Orders start at 6:00 p.m. tomorrow.

Derk looked weary as he stood silently watching the large gathering. There was a look of pain in his dark brown eyes. A groove appeared between his bushy eyebrows. His probing eyes, in the grip of deep emotion, tried to comprehend what the consequences of these orders would be for all those around him, and indeed the country as a whole. Derk turned around. He cast a worried look over the rowdy, visibly uneasy group of jeering people that surrounded him. The group turned quietly as if they expected an answer from their union leader.

The sight of this turmoil encouraged the already gloomy inclinations Derk had been wrestling with for a few days already. The uneasy feeling grew bigger deep inside him.

His face shadowed. *Oh, how I hate this dictator, Adolf Hitler! This man has caused so much death and turmoil already.* Derk's thoughts turned gloomy.

"What you thinking, boss? Come on! What you say?" Burly Jack fixed an impatient glare on Derk again. His eyes rolled wildly. "Tell us, man, tell us!" The group turned deathly quiet. Everyone knew their boss, Derk OpdenDries, never made big decisions in a hurry. They waited patiently.

With a firm set of his jaw, Derk started tapping his foot on the wet pavement in a steady rhythm. Big Jack groaned loud and clear. He extracted a big, crane-necked pipe from his side pocket. Jack held the pipe up high, then produced a worn-out pouch with home-grown tobacco. By the time Jack had filled the pipe bowl full of tobacco, Derk's foot quit tapping the pavement.

Derk's heart rate started to quicken as he tried to force a little smile at the corners of his mouth. But his eyes were void of joy. He straightened his shoulders. His honest, dark brown eyes searched the crowd standing around him.

He tried to clear his throat a few times, as if trying to find the right words. The crowd watched his face turn red, slowly but surely. The muscles in his face suddenly bunched up. His dark brown eyes narrowed to slits. Drops of perspiration broke out on his brow. His inner struggles exposed a series of facial movements. Derk remained silent, but only for a short moment before cresting into a thunderous reply. His eyes filled with anger in answer to their call.

"Let me tell each one of you! Never, ever shall this man, Derk OpdenDries, set foot on German soil to work in any of their factories and help build any guns, bombs, or weapons of war this evil dictator will employ to fight and kill our own citizens!" Derk's voice boomed loud and clear. "You will never, ever see the day when I lower myself to such vile and low-down, outrageous, inhumane tactics against a suffering people." His mouth trembled with anger. "That is all I have to say!"

Derk turned abruptly to make a quick exit. But his hurried exit did not sit well with Jack, who quickly followed Derk and grabbed him by the scruff of the neck, digging his nails into his shoulders one more time.

"Thanks, boss. Thanks so much." Jack's eyes expressed pure joy and satisfaction.

Derk opened his mouth as though to speak, then appeared to change his mind. He shoved Jack aside, grabbed his bike, and refused to answer any more questions as he brushed his way through the crowd to get to work.

The sun had sunk low, shining like a golden ball on the horizon, when Derk came home that day. It was near 5:30 when he opened the front door to his home. Derk took off his hat and hung it on one of the coat hangers by the front door. Grim-faced, he walked over to the bathroom sink to wash his hands. When he came into the kitchen, there loomed a solemn sadness around the supper table. There was not the usual happy atmosphere and chatter of his children. All was quiet. Derk took a quick glance around him. The supper table was bare, except for a huge pot of porridge Gerda had cooked up in plain water. The table was set with twelve empty porridge bowls, a spoon, and a glass of water beside each bowl. There was no milk, sugar, or syrup to sweeten the war-rationed meal. Nothing.

Derk sat down at the head of the table. He directed a searching look across the table at Gerda's bowed head. When she looked up, he noticed deep wrinkles forming on her otherwise smooth forehead. Strange, he'd never seen that before. Derk noticed a misty haze forming in her eyes.

"There was no bread, potatoes, or butter in the store today," Gerda said. Her eyes showed the hurt her lips would not reveal in front of her family sitting around the supper table. "I suppose we had all better learn to eat a little less." She forced a smile, trying to stay cheerful, but her usual bright blue eyes portrayed deep worry.

Derk shivered with sympathy. He walked over to Gerda and gently put his hands on her shoulders. "You know, there's plenty of God's grace to pull us through, Gerda. Let's hold on to His promises, shall we?" He spoke softly, yet with firm assurance. He turned to take his place at the head of the table once more. "Let us pray."

Derk uttered a humble prayer for help from above in all circumstances. Gerda received the new strength she was hoping for. With a soft smile, she started filling each bowl with a scoop of porridge. Derk watched in perfect silence. Everyone ate quietly.

All of a sudden, seven-year-old Jodi, with a round red face and long blond hair dangling down her shoulders, broke the silence with a sweet gentleness that showed in her dark blue eyes. "Seen the funniest thing happening today, Dad. There was about ten airplanes in the sky far away. I asked windmill boss, Mulder, if we could go on top of the flat part of the mill roof to see the planes zooming around, and you know what happened? Them dark looking airplanes threw out big things that looked like long cigars! It looked so funny, Dad. I counted twenty at least." Jodi's large dark grey eyes twinkled with sheer delight.

Johan, the second youngest son, who had a round walnut face and light blue eyes that people called "Jesus eyes," poked her in the ribs. He had serious mannerisms far beyond his twelve years. "It's not even funny at all, Dad. Mr. Mulder got mad at her, too. He said it would not be so funny if them big cigars landed on our town."

Derk looked across the table just in time to catch a glimpse of worry spread across his oldest son Josh's face. "Oh, by the way, Josh, Martin and Tom, I need to see you in my study right after supper. Important news. So be there, please."

Derk left the table after tasting some food off the near empty supper table. He went to his study, pulled out his desk chair, and sat down, torn with worry and fear. He cupped his head in his hands. He groaned, his deep hatred for this ruthless German dictator resurfacing once again, more fierce than ever before.

He was well aware that hatred was not a Christian virtue in the least. *But what about all the Jewish people, even the little children, that this selfish arrogant man has ordered to the gas chambers already? How can humanity put up with such evil deeds any longer?* Derk harboured no sympathy for Hitler's firm desire to rule the world on the principles of greed and self-interest alone. Derk's own worldview was so different. There was no comparison.

Never, ever will I begin to have any part in this evil scheme of conquering the world. Never! Derk stared into space. He wondered how he could communicate this message to his three sons with wisdom, without being too dominant.

Derk stood up and started pacing the floor a few times, then sat down. The weary "big-boss" folded his large work hands on top of the desk and yielded himself in deep hurt and humble heart. "Lord, I beg You, please send me Your wisdom to convey this message to my sons so that all I say and do will be pleasing in Your sight." Derk reached for the morning newspaper on the corner of his desk.

He heard quick footsteps down the hall. After a hasty knock, his office door opened wide. Josh, Martin, and Tom came into the office. Derk laid down his newspaper. His gaze lifted slowly from behind the oak desk. He looked up at his full grown sons.

"Say, Dad, did you see all those posters downtown today telling us to go work in Germany for the enemy? Are you gonna go for that, Dad? Are you?" Josh blurted out hastily.

Derk looked at Josh, his oldest son, and ran a hand through his dark hair. "I was going to discuss that with the three of you alone, Josh."

"I suppose the Germans expect us to help them fight this lousy war, Dad," Josh said. "What do you think we should do?"

On a sudden impulse, Derk jumped to his feet. He squared his shoulders and looked around the circle with dangerous calm. Then a sudden cry of anger rang though the room. "I've been thinking about this all day. Let's just be crystal clear about it all. Hitler expects each one of us to help him fight this awful war. This… this warped-minded creature demands us to cheerfully go and make weapons so he can use them to fight our own people!" Derk turned to walk off his frustration. "All of this is totally against everything I've ever stood and fought for."

Derk felt his nerves tighten. His face turned deep red. He struggled to find something encouraging to say. His usually kind face showed signs of deep anger in the fading rays of sunlight that peeked through the window in his office.

"Does that make sense to any of you?" He slammed his fist on the oak desk in front of him. His face portrayed the fury that was boiling inside of him. A determined look projected out his eyes. "Let me tell each one of you, once and for all, that never shall your father set one foot in any German factory to help the enemy build weapons for the purpose of killing a starving people, a people I love! None of you shall ever see the day come when I shall go work in Germany."

The boys saw determination engraved on their father's face. Derk's quivering lips, the withdrawn colour in his face, and the biting of his lower lip proved he meant business, even to the end of the war.

No more needed to be said.

"What will they do if we refuse to go?" Tom, the youngest of the three, burst out.

Derk recognized that he had to take control of his emotions. He sat down slowly, but his face turned to red once more. Derk arranged his hands like a little tent, fingertip to fingertip. He waited a moment to try to figure how best to present his views to his sons, then lifted his head slowly.

"Tom, that could mean sure death for any one of us. We may need to go into hiding soon, perhaps." He sighed. "I am afraid we could be in for a long and harsh war, boys."

"But who will feed the family if we have to go into hiding, Dad?" Josh's voice sounded worried.

Derk lifted his eyes upwards. "Heaven only knows." He spoke softly, firmly, and with sure conviction. "I have been watching the enemy soldiers at work for some time now. Some of them are pretty mean." He swallowed hard. "What's even worse, there are even some Dutch citizens who call themselves S.S. soldiers. They are traitors. Plain traitors! Hollanders, working for the enemy! Can you beat that?" Derk's sensitive brown eyes looked grim. His heart started racing once more. Somehow, he did manage to speak in a softer tone. "What any one of you want to do is your business," he said, looking at his young sons standing in front of him. "My decision will stand!"

Josh walked over to his dad. He put both hands on his shoulders. "I've been thinking a lot, Dad. I am gonna join the underground resistance movement today. Two of my best friends were already put in prison by the Germans a few weeks ago. I need to find a way to free them, Dad."

Josh expected a rebuke, a warning of danger from his dad. Instead, Derk's eyes started filling with tears. A pair of tears came trickling through both eyelashes and made a sort of crooked narrow pathway down his flushed cheeks.

But Josh was not about to give in to a few tears. "Listen, Dad," he said with irritation in his voice. "I'd be doing something to help my own citizens, my friends! I have to do that, Dad. Please, let me go." Josh's eyes were blazing with frustration.

Derk stood up ever so slowly. He placed a firm hand on Josh's shoulders, his eyes swimming with tears. "You know, Josh, I have been working in the resistance for a while myself. It is a risky business you're stepping into." His dark brown eyes pierced Josh's. "I respect you for your stand, son. You have my blessing." Derk felt a deep pride and thankfulness for his oldest son, who dared to stand up for the right things in life. He cleared his throat. "If you like, Josh, I can get you in touch with a few resistance workers right soon. Tonight, if you like."

Gerda come walking in the room.

"I'm glad you came, Gerda." Derk offered her a chair. "Now I can tell you all the latest news, too. Last night, at the underground resistance meeting, I heard about the very latest Nazi methods of searching down resistance workers. The Germans call it a *Razzia*."

The atmosphere in the room changed as if someone had clicked a switch. "What is a *Razzia*, Dad?" the boys asked in unison.

Sudden fear gripped Gerda's soul. She moved her lips as if to speak, but Derk lifted his hand, motioning her to be quiet a little longer. "In a *Razzia,* German soldiers conduct a sudden, unexpected raid. They try to find resistance workers and anyone voicing hatred against Hitler's army. They will come, break into homes, businesses, and any kind of building they feel like, any time of day or night. I am told they have already had great success in cities so far."

Derk tapped his right foot on the floor, a usual sign of his frustration. "And believe me, the hated S.S. soldiers, them traitors! They will not spare anybody, no man, woman, or child. That's the sad part." Derk glanced at Gerda sideways. He could not help but worry just how his wife would handle all this pressure. This was such a new way of life for all of them. Derk sensed urgency to prepare her. "Yes, Gerda, a *Razzia* could happen in this house, too. Trust me." Derk looked down at the floor, but only for a few seconds.

He looked up. With a resolute expression on his face, he directed a searching look at his three sons. The muscles in his solid jaw suddenly bunched up, and his eyes narrowed to slits. "Each of you better make up your own mind as to what you plan to do with the latest orders our friend Hitler hurled at us today." His voice sound defensive, bitter. "My own decision will stand!" Derk spoke louder then he meant to.

Tired, because the day had been hard on him, Derk rose up from his chair. He leaned both his hands on the edge of the desk. A soft, tired smile slid across his face as he looked at his sons. "Oh, by the way, will you help me find a way to make a few hiding places around here so no enemy can find us?" Then, Derk walked towards Gerda. "Shall we go see the rest of the family, Gerda?"

The two walked back into the living room. Hennie had put the four younger children to bed already.

Derk sat down by the round coffee table in the middle of the room, convinced that his sons would not report for work in Germany.

He picked up the evening newspaper and turned the page. The first thing he saw was Hitler's demands for all male citizens between eighteen and forty-five years to report for duty within the next two days. Half an hour later, Gerda brought him a cup of coffee made from surrogate coffee materials. There was no sugar or cream in it.

She sat down across from Derk. Derk looked up from reading the paper. "Hennie, will you help Mom find a way to shade the windows so that no light escapes to the outside?"

"But, Derk," Gerda said, searching his troubled eyes, "if the electricity is cut off at five o'clock each night, how can we have light anyhow?" She frowned. A deep sigh escaped her tight lips. "We've only got a dozen small candles left. They won't last for more than two weeks at best, Derk. What can we do for lighting?"

Without a trace of doubt in his voice, Derk replied, "I am sure our sons will figure out a way to build a lighting device for the winter."

Derk heard fast footsteps in the hallway. Josh, Martin, and Tom came into the living room. They looked cheerful.

"We thought of a couple of ideas, Dad," said Tom, the husky broad-shouldered boy with the usually smiling eyes. "First thing early in the morning we will go and make a couple of hiding places. One inside the house upstairs, and another under the rabbit cages in the shed outside."

"How will you make a hiding place where all four of you can hide yourselves in this small house?" Gerda asked.

"Oh, we'll go cut a hole behind the closet in Tom and Martin's bedroom," Josh suggested. "We can squeeze into the side of the sloping side of the roof. They'll never find us if we can get there in time."

"Sounds interesting," Derk said. "What about for the one outside?"

Tom's eyes glistened with pride. "We'll dig a big hole under Johan's rabbit cages—so we can quickly jump inside when they come looking for us. We'll have to train Bert, Johan and Dick, our little brothers, to take turns pushing the rabbit cages back in place once we're down there. They'll never find us, Dad."

"We'd be running out of oxygen mighty quick, wouldn't you think?" asked Derk. "How would you get fresh air to come in from the outside, boys?"

"We thought about that, too. All we need to do is lead a long stove pipe into the hole from the outside. We'll hide the pipe amongst the tall grass on the back of the shed," Martin explained.

Derk nodded his head. "Could work. I'm sure it could."

"We'll do all the work at night, so the neighbours won't find out, either. Can't trust anybody in this war, Dad. Nobody!" Solemn fear shone in Josh's eyes, as though he'd had an experience of some sort already.

The OpdenDries family together mapped out a solid plan for their future. They heard the church clock strike twelve o'clock midnight.

3

Razzia!

It was a mild sunny day in late September 1943. The grass was still green and the flowerbeds were ablaze with a mass of daisies, snap dragons, and dahlias. Up the face of the red brick-covered front of the house, with the freshly painted white window sills, climbed ivy-leaved geraniums and a clematis which each spring in May produced a riot of pale lilac-coloured flowers. Clusters of pink, purple, yellow, and bronze mums were in full bloom, extending their floral beauty for anyone to enjoy when passing by the OpdenDries' neatly kept yard.

It was 5:30 in the afternoon. Derk sat by the living room table, poised intently over the morning's newspaper. The whole family was home. Gerda and their nineteen-year-old daughter Hennie were busy making supper ready in the kitchen.

Derk had felt an uneasy feeling all day. A friend had told him that the Germans had mastered great successes with several *Razzia* raiding parties in other parts of the town over the past few days.

Derk rose to his feet. He called a meeting with all his family before supper. With deep probing eyes, Derk looked around the circle. "Things are getting mighty scary out there. The Germans are squeezing the noose around our necks, so to speak," he cautioned.

Derk sat down. He let out a deep sigh and turned reflective. "The war is heading towards the fifth year now," he said, consumed with worries for his family. "Hitler has murder on his mind. We need to accept that as a fact of this war. Hitler is a blatant murderer. Look how many Jews he's already sent to the gas chambers. Men, woman, and even little children!" Derk's eyes reflected true sadness.

"Oh, but Dad, we'll look after ourselves as a family," said Josh, with a bold, daring look, unafraid.

"I know, son, I know. That's what your mother and I expect of each of you. But there's so much more to think of, Josh." Serene silence filled the room. Derk stood up. He put his hands in his pockets. The responsibility for the safety and welfare of his family weighed heavily on his shoulders.

Derk made a soft scraping noise in his throat. He threw up his dark head of hair, sensing that he needed to take charge of the situation in a calm manner. "First thing we need to do is plan security measures in case trouble comes our way. Boys, I want each of you to take a turn standing by the window as a spy person, starting this very moment. Keep a close eye to see if you see any German soldiers coming down the road. If so, holler!"

Thirteen-year-old Sid asked, "Can I stand guard first, Dad, please?" He had the typical self-confidence of a young teenager. It glowed from his good-looking, smooth, round face. Ten minutes into his watch, a certain impatience shadowed his firm-set youthful features. Sid kept walking back and forth by the window as if to ease his inner feelings. He suddenly stopped and started staring down the road, shadowing his eyes with both his hands.

"Mom, there's a bunch of soldiers coming down the road." His voice sounded nervous. "They stopped by the neighbours, Mom. I see two S.S. men. Hurry! Tell Dad! Oh, there's another five coming down the sidewalk through the garden up front." Sid turned to look at Gerda.

Gerda looked at her second youngest son, Johan, so young, so afraid. She stopped dishwashing abruptly, her attention caught by the anxious tone in Sid's voice.

"*Razzia!*" she murmured, more to herself than to her son. Her eyes danced helplessly, but only for a few seconds before she ran into the living room, wiping her wet hands on her apron. "Derk! Boys! *Razzia!*" She uttered that dreaded word while pointing her finger at the front door. "They're heading for the front. Hurry! Get out! All of you! Hide. Outside. Quick!"

The boys needed no further explanation. Earlier in the day, the family had started rehearsing for just this type of emergency. Each jumped to their feet, neatly piling their books in a bookcase nearby.

Derk immediately started calculating the situation. There was no way they could get into the hiding place upstairs they had just finished yesterday. Any noise from upstairs would alert the soldiers.

"Quick. Outside," whispered Derk. "Hurry!"

The foursome slipped out the back door. They could hear loud banging noises on the heavy oak front door. Gerda and Sid started scanning the room for any trace Derk and the boys might have left behind a moment ago. But Hennie, instantly aware of the tense situation, had already hidden the coffee mugs in the back of the kitchen cupboard. She had a stern face illumined by unusually dark eyes instead of the friendly expression she usually wore.

Gerda leisurely turned a few pillows on the coach, just to gain a few extra minutes. The banging on the door grew louder, sharper, like a crashing sound. One of the soldiers turned his rifle and with the butt of his rifle started hammering the thick door hard and heavy.

Gerda walked slowly to the front door and felt an unexplainable calm come over her.

She opened the door as though in slow motion. Before the door was half-opened, four soldiers with their heavy boots came barging inside. The soldiers at once started searching room by room. The fifth, a tall, broad-shouldered masculine figure with thin cheeks and cold, pale blue eyes, parked himself in the doorway. His cumbersome presence filled most of the opening. He had bright yellow S.S. letters sewn onto his collar.

He towered over Gerda, looking down at her with a roguish grin on his rough red face. He began strutting around aggressively. "Your spouse and three boys are hiding in this house?" The man spoke with an irritating raspy voice and eyes void of compassion. "We know they're here!" The man spoke Dutch fluently.

Gerda lifted a level gaze in his direction that had something of disbelief in them. Her hands balled into fists as she flashed the soldier a defiant look. Gerda's body stiffened at the thought of the sheer brutality of this man to set foot in her house and go searching for his own people, his own countrymen! *Traitor*! That was all she could think at the moment.

Gerda felt blood rushing to her cheeks but managed to pull herself together. After a purposeful delay, Gerda squared her shoulders. The tiny brave mother looked like a gallant tiger ready to crunch her prey at a moment's notice. A muscle quivered in her face. She shot a piercing, deadly gaze in his direction with fire in her eyes. *You traitor!* Gerda seethed inside. She looked down and remained silent momentarily, then lifted a determined cool, calm gaze to meet the hate-filled stare of this Dutch brute shadowing the doorway. The set expression of her eyes and mouth told an eloquent story of grit and determination.

Gerda took a deep breath. Straightening her shoulders, she dug both of her fists into her sides confidently. She moved squarely in front of this towering S.S. soldier who stood looking down on her with a sarcastic grin on his face. She could smell his bad breath. With a stubborn set of the jaw, Gerda nearly screamed, "It seems to me, you Dutchman, that you should be able to find a better job than wasting your time and energy betraying your own people! Your countrymen!" Gerda managed a fake sheepish grin. *Oh, how I long to slap him in the face!*

The S.S. soldier's narrow eyes turned wild with fury. His lips moved momentarily, his jaws jutting slightly, as if he did not know how to answer Gerda's sharp remark. Then he took a giant step in Gerda's direction, seething under his breath. His nostrils widened and started flaring back and forth. Stamping the butt of his rifle on the kitchen floor irritably, the soldier took a step closer in Gerda's direction.

Towering over her, the S.S. soldier screamed in Gerda's face, "Madam, where are they? Your sweetheart! Your sons! Where are they hiding?"

Gerda stepped aside calmly. With a grim smirk on her face, she made a waving motion. "Why, come on in. Take a look for yourselves."

The soldier worked up a sickly smile and grabbed Gerda by the neck. He crashed both her shoulders into the wall, then, with a cold nod in her direction, went stomping up the stairs where he watched his soldiers bang three young children up against the wall.

Johan and Bert, Jodi's two youngest brothers, stood huddled against the wall with Jodi in the middle. Jodi cried softly. A wide, wicked grin framed the S.S. man's face as he watched his soldiers tear apart beds and punch holes in the mattresses with their bayonets. Dawn feathers spread all over the beds and the floors of the four bedrooms.

One soldier crashed a closet door with his heavy boot. Another smashed two chairs across the foot end of a bed, breaking them to pieces. "Nothing. Nothing here!" he shouted. "Found nothing in this house!" He rushed down the stairs, as if his life depended on it, motioning the others to follow. Together they rushed wildly through the kitchen.

"Over there!" The first soldier pointed his fingers towards an old shed outside. They all rushed towards the back of the house where Derk kept a milk cow, like many other households did. The front soldier kicked out the back door and raced towards the shed where Derk and the boys were hiding.

It had only been five minutes since Derk and his three sons had slid into the cold, wet hiding place under the rabbit cages in the shed. Marcel, one year below the compulsory eighteen-year age limit for the work camps, had run up ahead of them and grabbed the rabbit cage. Quick as lightning, he'd yanked ever so hard on the handle of the secret door. Marcel's heavy pull, though, had exposed a two-by-three foot opening that led into the hiding place. Derk and the boys had slid down into the hole in snake-like fashion.

Marcel shoved open the door on top of the hole and grabbed a handful of fresh hay to put it in the rabbit cage. He carefully moved the rabbit cage back in place and slowly sauntered over to the basketball court in the backyard. Marcel started shooting baskets.

He saw the soldiers come storming out of the house as if the house was set on fire. The S.S. man grabbed hold of Marcel. "Where's your dad and brothers?" he demanded.

Marcel looked up into the soldier's fanatic, beady little eyes. Marcel felt no fear inside of him. He fixed an unblinking stare up at the soldier, his lips quivering with indignation. His black button eyes flared with anger as they pierced into the traitor's cold-hearted face.

"You are a Dutchman, aren't you? A traitor!" Marcel spat on the ground. The S.S. released his grip and slapped Marcel in the face.

The soldier shook him unmercifully, then threw him to the ground hard. "There! Shut your mouth, you miserable little creature!" He kicked Marcel in the ribs with his heavy boots.

Gerda watched the whole scene develop right in front of her. She clasped her hands anxiously in front of her. "Oh, Lord," she sighed. "Guard Derk and all our family, please?"

Marcel struggled to get to the house, bent over in pain. Hatred reflected like a mirror in his deep blue eyes. "I hate that man, Mom. I hate him!" He nearly cried. Gerda ran up the stairs to see her three youngest children. Johan, Bert, and Jodi stood cowering with large frightened eyes in the far corner of the room paralyzed with fear. The children were shivering and crying with fear, staring at the mess the soldiers had left behind.

Gerda quickly ran over to them. She put her arm around them and hugged all three at once. "You're safe now. Don't worry no more," she whispered, holding them close to her. She gave each an extra little squeeze to try reassuring them. "Come, follow me. Hurry." They all ran down the narrow stairway to see what was happening to the rest of the family outside. Gerda stood by the back porch window to get a quick look towards the shed where the soldiers had gone into. Gerda nearly froze when she saw the four soldiers come out of the shed. A few started moving the dead grasses at the back of the shed with the butts of their rifles.

Oh, Lord! Gerda sighed. *Guard the boys and their father. I beg of You, Father up above, please!*

The usually quiet-tempered Dick had been watching the whole affair with fear in his heart. "They'll be looking for a disguised entrance somewhere, Mom," he said.

Together they watched the soldiers gather in a circle right above the hole where Derk and the boys were hiding. One of the soldiers pounded the butt of his rifle on the ground. Gerda's heart started skipping wildly. All of a sudden, the S.S. man shouted out a loud order and the soldiers marched away at a brisk trot towards the neighbour's house.

Gerda walked outside. Satisfaction glistened on her face. She walked over to Marcel once more and put her arms around his shoulders. Marcel lifted his head to look at her. "That one man was a Dutchman, Mom," Marcel spoke with sad eyes. "I hate him."

Gerda waited for a moment, pondering how to reply. A deep sigh escaped her tight lips. "The Lord's been keeping us safe this far, Marcel. Let's be thankful for all of that, shall we?" She swallowed a big lump in her throat. "I know there will be better days, Marcel. Maybe soon, let's hope."

Gerda's own thankfulness shone through by the way she looked at her son.

Little Jodi's anxious voice broke the strange silence. "Mom, the soldiers are gone now, aren't they? Gone forever, Mom?" Jodi shivered like a leaf from the ordeal they were forced to go through.

Bert, Jodi's youngest brother, put his arms around Jodi's shoulders. Bert tried to sound grown up. "Don't you worry, Jodi. Your brothers will watch out for you. Trust me." His sweet round face smiled down at her.

Gerda put Jodi's hand in hers. Dick took her other hand and squeezed it lightly. "Don't you worry, little sister. You got lots and lots of big brothers. They will take care of you, always." Dick puffed up his chest to look manlier.

Hennie and Sid stood in the doorway to stop the younger ones from going outside. Marcel had gone upstairs, but now he came down in a hurry. "Mom, it's just awful upstairs. The soldiers smashed all our beds to pieces. There's feathers all over the place!" His eyes shot full of tears. "Those soldiers are a mean bunch, Mom. I want to kill them. All of them!"

Gerda felt a lump forming in her throat again. She could not answer him at once. Her heart began to realize just how much this raid had affected her children emotionally, as well as psychologically.

And how many more razzias will there be, Lord? Gerda sighed in despair. She put her arms around the two youngest ones and tried to smile. "Dad and the boys will try to fix up the beds again." She hugged the little ones. "Try not to worry." She herself was not convinced at all that Derk and the boys had the nerve to stay home any longer. This had been the second raid this year already.

Gerda walked over to Marcel and Sid, her eyes glistening in tears. "Thanks for being such a big help, boys. Thanks."

Marcel sensed the seriousness of the situation. "Do you think Dad and the boys will be alright, Mom?" he whispered softly.

Gerda stroked her tired forehead. "Thank God they are for now." She looked at Marcel. "Please go tell Dad to stay in the hiding place for a while. We just never know if they'll come back tonight, do we?"

Late that evening, Derk spoke with tinged sadness, "I think we may have to leave and find another place to hide, Gerda. It's not safe here for us anymore." Derk kept a steady eye on her face as he made the remark. He saw Gerda's expression stiffen into wariness, alert with fear.

Gerda groaned softly. *I am convinced that no matter what will happen to any one of us, the sun will rise once again for us someday.*

She rose from her chair, then walked towards Derk, who was standing by the living room easy chair. "You must do what you figure is best for us all, Derk," she said. "I trust you."

She gave Derk a heartfelt kiss.

4

Bad News

June 12, 1944 dawned clear and warm with a bright blue sky and just enough breeze to promise a pleasant day.

Thirteen-year-old Sid tried to concentrate on his homework, but instead he watched shiny bright sunrays teasingly play shadow tricks across the kitchen table. He shifted around on his chair and glanced up at the clock on the wall. "Sick!" It was four o'clock in the afternoon. He slammed his arithmetic book shut.

He slipped on his jacket, grabbed his hard rubber-wheeled bicycle, and biked down Mill Street towards the densely wooded forest near the edge of town. He felt excited to be venturing all on his own for the very first time in his life.

Good thing school was bombed down last week, otherwise I'd be sitting in school and not able to bike around the town.

Sid knew that his dad would not have approved of him going into the woods all by himself with the war going on, but it was only a fifteen-minute bike ride to get there. He was not afraid. He knew he could find his way home in no time, even if it was pitch dark outside. He and his brother Dick had gone wandering through the woods tons of times.

Once Sid came to what he called "the forest," he stepped down off his bike and quickly shoved it under a thick layer of low-hanging branches. He glanced back down the road.

Yep! Nobody will find this treasure of mine. He grinned, gently stroking the back fender of his bike as if it were a soft little kitten.

Sid crouched down low and worked his way through small bushes towards the cleared area. He heard voices nearby. He slid on his tummy, inching cautiously towards where the sounds were coming from. The voices grew louder, filled with excitement. Sid kept crawling forward, as far as he dared to go. He pushed back a few branches to make a hole that he could peek through, then lifted up his head.

Sid was stunned at what he saw. His mouth hung open, his eyes alert with wide wonder. *Wow! Fifty soldiers, lined up along both sides of some kind of runway. Must be important!*

Before he get could any closer, he heard a massive truck approaching. Sid felt glued to the ground. The soldiers suddenly grew silent as they watched the truck drive onto an unloading ramp. Next to the ramp stood another contraption that looked like a long cement launch pad of some sort, the same kind he had read about in a book at school a few weeks ago. It had sort of a buggy with wheels attached to it, too.

Sid watched, spellbound, as the truck drove up to a big ramp. Two soldiers jumped out of the vehicle and let down the tailgate. Sid heard squeaky noises as he gazed at a huge, round piece of metal that looked like a big cigar with wings hitched on top of what looked like an airplane. Another four big cigar-like objects were stored in a huge shed away from the launching pad.

Sid felt a sudden urge to go home and tell his dad about his latest discovery. He crawled on his stomach back to his bike, jumped back on, and feverishly raced back home. He knew his dad would give him a good scolding, but wow… this was important news.

Once home, Sid dumped his bike on the sidewalk and peeked through the kitchen window. He saw that his mom had supper on the table already. Sid wanted to blurt out the news so badly he could hardly wait until everyone was seated around the table. He bit his tongue. He waited for his dad to say grace.

I'm sure everyone will be proud of my discovery. I just know it. Wow!

Supper was the usual big pot of potato soup. Sid wiggled on his chair as his mom scooped the soup into the bowls. The bigger the person, the more soup she gave them. There was not much left for Mom and Jodi at the end, but then Jodi did not care much anyhow. She'd been eating this kind of soup for such a long, long time that she really did not care to have more than a little bit.

When Gerda was finished filling all the soup bowls, Sid could not wait any longer.

"Guess what I saw today, Dad?"

Derk looked at Sid sitting across the table. He saw Sid lift his curly blond head, looking straight up at him. His eyes glittered with excitement. Sid squinted both eyelids, as if he had discovered the greatest invention ever.

"Where did you go out to explore today, Sid?" Derk questioned, knowing the adventurous mind of his ambitious thirteen-year-old son.

Sid tried to neglect the serious tone in Derk's voice. He felt all his brothers looking at him.

Sid puffed out his chest and lifted his chin. "Oh, I've seen some important stuff, Dad—in the bush where Dick and me have been going for a long time." Sid took a deep breath. "And you know what, Dad? They were unloading some big, long things that looked like great big cigars. Must be a bunch of bombs, eh, Dad?"

Gerda saw the colour drain out of Derk's face, a slight tremor of the mouth and jowl. The wrinkles in his forehead deepened.

Derk did not reply for a moment. He decided not to reprimand his son. "What did the soldiers look like, Sid?"

"Oh, they had lots of decorations on their uniforms, Dad. A couple of them had real shiny gold trim on bands around their necks. A few had S.S. on their collars, too. They are betrayers, Dad, I know. I read about them."

Derk raised his eyebrows. He remained silent. He thought of the article in the *Dutch Intelligence* he had read the day before. Could these be the dreaded V-1 missiles he'd read about? They were the first ever guided cruise missiles, eight metres long, that Hitler planned to use as low flying bombs to destroy London. Derk stared out the window, a worried look shadowing his tired looking face.

Sid had no time to wait for an answer. "You think they'll be using these bombs on us, Dad?"

A heavy atmosphere shrouded the room. Derk looked around the table. He saw faces full of fear, young children staring wide-eyed into a world they did not yet understand. Derk cleared his throat. "These missiles are meant to help destroy London, England Sid. It's a wicked way of waging war. I don't think they will be used to bomb Holland any-time soon, son." Derk cast a shadowed look at Sid across the table.

Next day, the very first V-1 missile was sent to London, England from the launch base that Sid had discovered the day before, in Nyverdal, in the heart of Holland.

5

Stray V-1 Missile

Small tufts of sheep-like clouds hastily moved along, making room for an umbrella of twinkling little stars in the heavenly firmament above. Derk jumped over a few small ditches and snuck down five narrow back roads. The twinkling stars above were the only light to help him find his way to the Dutch Underground Resistance meeting at a friend's place.

Derk stopped for a moment, looking up to enjoy the bright, sparkling stars in the universe high above. A smile slid across his face. Hitler's orders for complete darkness could not stop the twinkling heavenly glory from instilling a little bit of cheer in the hearts of a heavily burdened people bent low under a ruthless dictatorship. It felt as if the Lord up in heaven spoke softly, "Fear not, I am with thee, always."

It was September 5, 1944.

Eight-year-old Jodi peddled for dear life on an upside-down bicycle to help provide just a little bit of light in the living room. The heavy window curtains were drawn tightly shut. It was eight o'clock in the evening.

Gerda quietly observed Jodi's happy face as she tried peddling and making shadow faces on the wall at the same time. A smile crossed Gerda's tired face. "Them creative sons of ours!" she said.

Earlier that day, Tom had come marching into the house with his bicycle. He looked like a hero. "I think I got it figured out, Mom." Tom then turned his bike upside-down and started moving the peddles. The battery-operated headlight provided enough light to read a book by.

"Wow! We can even play games and stuff with this light, Mom," Martin exclaimed. "Great, Tom! Guess we should figure out a way to invent a proper seat on the up-side-down bicycle, right?"

When Gerda tucked little Bert and Jodi into bed that night, Bert asked, "Mom, are there going to be a lot of big dark clouds in the sky tonight"

"I don't know, Bert. Why do you ask?"

"When it's dark, the airplanes can't find our place to bomb, Mom. Don't you see?"

Tears stung the back of Gerda's eyes. She lifted her eyes up heavenwards. *Why, Lord? Why do children so small need to be so afraid?* A deep sigh escaped her trembling lips. *How long, Lord? How much longer must we suffer?* She wiped a falling teardrop away from her eyes with the back of her hand. *I just don't know how much longer I can take this hunger, this fear, Lord. Please help us.*

Instead of dwelling on these thoughts any longer, Gerda said, "We'd best go pray now."

"Yeah, let's go pray for the whole, wide world," Bert echoed.

Gerda put their small hands inside hers. She swallowed around a big lump in her throat and expressed a deep cry for freedom, not just for her own family, but for the whole world.

"Night now, Bert. Night, Jodi. Remember, the Lord way up in the sky is watching over all of us all the time. Don't be afraid anymore."

Bert turned to look at her. "Even Josh and Dad, Mom? Why have they not come home yet?"

Gerda skilfully ignored Bert's question, but only for the peace of mind of her little ones. "Yes, Bert, even Josh and Dad. Trust me."

Derk came home at ten o'clock that evening from a resistance meeting. He looked pale and tired.

Derk sighed. "Maybe we should go to bed now, Gerda."

"But Josh hasn't come home yet, Derk."

"He'll come home later. They planned a little surprise for the Germans, Gerda. Trust me, these ten young resistance fighters know what they're doing. They're a brave bunch, Gerda. I am proud of our son."

Gerda heard Josh come home around midnight. Even after that, she had a hard time falling asleep. She looked at the clock on her bedside table. It was two o'clock in the morning. She laid down her head on the pillow once more. Derk was fast asleep.

She suddenly heard a low rumbling noise in the far distance. It was coming closer. The noise grew louder, as if it were heading straight towards her. Gerda jumped out of bed. The rumbling grew into a thundering crescendo, like a huge chorus. It seemed to pass right over their rooftop. Gerda let out a holler. "Derk, wake up!"

Derk had already woken. He jumped out of bed, instantly. All the children came scrambling down the stairs. Bert and Jodi flew into Gerda's arms.

"What's that awful noise?" Everyone shouted at once.

Derk quickly dressed and ran to the living room window. He shoved aside the curtains and stared out the window to check if he could see anything in the sky at all. The rumbling noise slowly faded. A long streak of light made a huge circle in the far distance.

The four oldest boys—Josh, Tom, Martin, and Marcel—stood outside. They had also seen this unusual flying object. All they could see now, though, was a long tail of bright light passing overhead.

Marcel's voice quivered with fear, "I wonder if it will come back."

"Funniest noise I've ever heard," Tom muttered under his breath. "Spooky."

"Well, it's gone now. Might as well go to bed again," said Martin, the everlasting optimist. He turned to go inside. The rest followed.

Suddenly, Josh said, "Quiet!" He cupped his hand around his ear and held the right side of his face against the front window pane. "Uh-oh! I hear the rumbling again!"

Everyone listened intently.

"Come," Josh said, motioning his brothers. "Put your ear to the window."

"Is it a V-1?" Derk muttered, more to himself than anyone else. "Come on, we might as well get dressed."

Marcel raced up the stairs, dressed, and came hurrying down again. The noise was deafening. Everyone covered their ears.

"I think it's louder than the first time, don't you, Dad?" Josh shouted, trying to be heard above the rumbling.

Derk whizzed past the boys and went out the kitchen door. His sons followed him. In the clear, twinkling sky under a full moon they saw a long streak of fire come out of the tail-end of what looked like an airplane zooming low over the rooftops. Derk turned his head slowly, following the streak of fire disappear into the distance. Fear stained his face. *Oh, no! There it is again. No mistake about it… it's a V-1 for sure!* He groaned out loud.

They could hear loud talking all around. People stood outside their homes looking up into the sky, waiting for the next round of missiles to come through. The whole town was up in arms.

Derk and all his sons continued scanning the horizon. Josh stood beside him.

"I think it's the V-1 missile, used by the *Luftwaffe* to bomb England," Josh said. "Must be one of the first ones propelled from the launch pad in our town." Josh sounded confident, sure of himself. "They zoom along at 360 miles an hour, carry three-quarter tons of high explosives, and can go as far as 235 miles. They're operated by an automatic pilot." Josh shifted his feet. "Once in a while, something goes wrong with the pilot mechanisms. Then you get a stray missile, like this one, scaring the daylights out of people. Hitler calls it his 'Retaliation Weapon.'" Josh's voice sounded bitter and he clenched his fists. "If we could only do something, Dad. Anything!"

Derk was aware that Josh and his resistance group had studied how the V-1 missiles actually operated. Derk looked up at his oldest son, who was taller than him. Parked under the millions of sparkling stars, he noticed deep despair marked on Josh's ever so young face.

The other boys ran to the back of the house, trying to spot the coming missile.

Sid's voice was filled with anticipation. "Dad, Josh, come quick! I think it's coming back again." His eyes glittered with excitement.

Derk nod soberly as the V-1 made yet another pass over the town, flying far too close to the rooftops for his liking. He nudged Josh's side. "What will happen, Josh?"

Josh cleared his throat. "It will keep circling until it runs out of fuel. You never know where it will hit, Dad. It's awful scary, don't you think?"

"How long will that take, you think?"

A sigh escaped Josh's tight held lips. "It could take up to four hours, at least. A long time. Too long." Josh's shoulders drooped in despair.

Derk knew it would be a long night for all of them. "I'll go tell Gerda and the rest to get dressed. It may be a long night for all of us." With that, Derk went inside.

Josh walked to the back of the house, joining his brothers. "Boys, we better get prepared, just in case something happens close by."

Young Johan's eyes were big and full of fear. "Why? What's gonna happen, Josh?"

Josh pointed up to the sky. "Watch that big beast of an airplane come again. It's one of the first jet-powered cruise missiles. The Germans launch them from right here in town. They send them to attack England. But every once in a while, one goes astray. That's what's happened to this one."

"So, you think it will hit our town when it runs out of fuel, Josh?" asked Tom, the engineer in the family.

Josh waited to answer until the missile roared above them once more. "Could be anywhere. Wherever it does land, it will cause more damage than a bomb. Let's pray it won't happen here in the middle of town." Josh looked over his seven brothers. A lump formed in his throat. His face lifted heavenward. "Please, Lord. Save all of us, please?" He sighed.

Derk found Gerda sitting in a big chair near the fireplace, hugging Jodi on her lap. Hennie sat right beside her. When the missile passed over again, Gerda shivered visibly. She tried to rearrange her emotions into some kind of harmonious order in front of Derk and the children. Everyone cringed for the thirty-fifth time under the thundering noise overhead.

Resolute, Derk stepped outside. He ordered all the boys to come inside and get down on their knees around Gerda's chair. "Best do some heavy praying, right now!" Derk said with a firm voice. Derk put Gerda and Jodi's small hands into his own strong hands. He closed his eyes, begging for divine protection for all of them and the rest of the village.

Jodi squeezed her eyes shut. She could not really understand all the big words her dad used, but as far as she was concerned they could stand to receive a whole lot of help from somewhere!

The family sat through the long night. Townsfolk were buzzing until the first golden sunrays lit the horizon. The feared flying bomb zoomed over once more, began sputtering right above the OpdenDries' home, then made a sharp descent near the outskirts of town. Panic set in amongst the town's citizens. Everybody ran for shelter.

"Get under the table, all of you!" Derk hollered.

Seconds later, a blinding flash of vibrant red, yellow, and orange merged into a symphony of colours. The heavens echoed a dreadful, thunderous noise one last time while death stretched out its fingers towards seven innocent citizens living on a farm where it had gone down.

6

Little Anne

The sun slipped its last golden, crimson edge behind the clouds. It had been a warm, sunny day in July. Jodi stood in the doorway of her friend's house, waiting for eight-year-old Anne Belinsky to come play with her outside.

Jodi was awfully upset. Dad, Josh, Martin, and Tom had left home last night. "They are in hiding from Hitler's soldiers," Mom had said. Maybe they'd only be gone for a little while.

But how does Mom know when they will come home again? How can she tell?

Jodi shivered. Her friends were scared all the time of missiles and bombings. She shifted from one foot to the other. Maybe, just maybe, Mom was right. She always was.

Johann Mulder, known as the friendly boss in the windmill, sat by the kitchen table munching on a piece of toast with egg. He was reading the paper casually.

Jodi looked at the toast and eggs that was set in front of Johann Mulder. Oh, the smell of fried eggs gave rise to sharp, aching pains in the pit of her stomach—the same kind of pain that kept her awake at night lots of times. The colour drained from her face. Jodi's dark, starry eyes reflected her longing for just a tiny piece of toast. *Just a wee little bite would be so good.*

Jodi bit her lip. It started bleeding. She quickly wiped away the blood with the back of her hand.

Mom had told her that the funny feelings in her stomach were hunger pains, because there was not enough food in her stomach. Her eyes started wandering through the room. There, on the kitchen countertop, she saw a half-loaf of white bread. Her mouth started watering. Oh, the pain in her stomach hurt so bad. Jodi squeezed both her eyes shut. Maybe for supper Mom would have some bread just like Johann was eating right now. Jodi bit her lip again. She looked as if she wanted to say something. Instead, she began to count to ten like Mom had taught her to do, and looked out the kitchen window. Her stomach ached.

Jodi heard sudden footsteps along on the gravel path beside the house. The noise shook her out of her dream world. It was sixteen-year-old Marcel, her brother. Marcel was in too much of a hurry to pay any attention to his little sister. He was on a mission! He rushed past her, shouting loudly so that the Jewish family Mulder had hiding upstairs, the Belinskys, could hear him.

"*Razzia!* Hurry!" Marcel waved both his arms to Johann Mulder.

The miller boss quickly jumped to his feet. Before his feet touched the ground, Marcel had already disappeared around the corner to warn the next neighbours all the way down the street.

Johann ran up the stairway. He felt awfully sorry for Jodi, who was waiting for her friend Anne, but at the same time he had to take care of his own family's needs first.

This was the first time a *Razzia* had come to his home. He knew they would come looking for Jews to send to the gas chambers sooner or later. Johann was well aware that if the Germans were to find any Jews hiding at his place, he could be shot to death.

Johann hurried to help hide the four members of the Belinsky family in the attic of their small home. Halfway up the stairs, he saw little Anne, the nine-year-old little Jewish girl, come bouncing down the stairs. "I am gonna play with Jodi, Johann."

But kind old Johann stopped Anne. "Later, Anne, later!" he whispered urgently.

Anne knew what to expect already. Her mom had told her lots of time. But Anne let out fierce holler. "I don't want to hide, Uncle Johann!" She struggled against Johann's firm grip, trying to make her escape. "It's awfully dark in the attic. I hate it up there! Let me go!" She kicked Johann's shins with her wooden shoes.

Johann's wife Minnie was upstairs already, warning the family to hide. She came running down. She paused to catch her breath and calm her pounding heart.

Johann hung on to the struggling Anne, holding her tight. He threw a quick glance at Jodi. "Go get your mom, Jodi! Tell her to come help us, quick!"

Jodi turned and ran all the way home. Her wooden shoes went clip-clop, clip-clop on the hard pavement. She could hear Anne scream above the noise of her wooden shoes.

Gerda saw Jodi come running home wildly. Her heart jumped and she ran to meet Jodi at the door. "What happened anyhow?"

"Mom, Mom! Johann says, *Razzia!*" She stamped the toe of her wooden shoe on the pavement to signal the urgency of her message.

Gerda knew there was not a moment to spare. She quick slipped on her shoes and hurried across the road. Jodi ran inches behind her.

When Gerda came to the doorway, she saw Johann struggling with the little Jewish girl with pitch-black hair, telling her to hurry back upstairs. Anne kept yelling, "I want to play with Jodi, Uncle Johann! Let me go!"

Gerda sized up the situation calmly. She noticed a couple of toques hanging by the outside door. She grabbed hold of the headwear. "Hold it, Johann. Let Anne go outside with Jodi and have a game of football with the other children in the backyard of the windmill."

She gently took the girl by the hand. "Come, Anne. You go play with Jodi. She's been waiting for you a long time already outside." Gerda put the red toque over her black hair and shoved her black curly hair under the rim. Gerda's eyes filled with compassion. She pulled the little girl close to her side and looked down at Anne, who lifted her chin towards her. "No more crying now, do you hear, Anne?"

Anne quit crying. She raced out in the cold autumn air to have a game of soccer with Jodi and her brothers on the old windmill yard.

Jodi raced after her. Gerda grabbed hold of her young daughter just before she slipped out the door. "Here, Jodi, you wear this toque until the *Razzia* is over. You understand?"

Jodi's eyes widened with child-like trust in which there was no scepticism. "But it's not cold outside at all."

Oh, how can I make her understand the seriousness of our problem? Gerda hugged her little girl. "Jodi, please understand, with Anne wearing a toque over her black hair, the soldiers won't notice she's a Jewish girl. You don't want her to have to go away from here, do you?"

Jodi lifted her sensitive eyes towards Gerda, as if she comprehended the critical nature of their predicament. "All right, Mom." Pulling her toque a little further over her ears, Jodi raced outside to play football with Anne and her brothers.

"Will you let me and Anne be the goalies today?" she screeched to her brothers, kicking the ball they had made from a pig's bladder the day before.

"Yep," said Dick. "Anne, you stand in this goal here. Jodi, you stand in the other goal. And Anne, don't cry no more, you hear me?"

Jodi was happy. She had long since learned that it was much easier to be a goalie than getting your legs kicked all the time by those hard wooden shoes. And some of those shoes even had wires around them to keep the wooden parts together. Those wired-up shoes hurt a lot!

Gerda barely managed to make it back to her own home when three soldiers come barging in. "We're looking for Jews," an S.S., soldier said in fluent Dutch.

Gerda was not worried in the least. Derk and the boys had gone into hiding a few months earlier. They were far away from civilization, digging peat blocks and drying them in the sun for people to use in the winter for heating their houses. They made very little money, but it was enough that the family might survive the winter—assuming they could get the money back to Gerda.

These particular soldiers did not disturb the bedding or break the beds this time. They did not seem the least bit interested in finding anybody. *Had a good bunch this time. Thank the good Lord!* Gerda lifted her gaze towards heaven.

A deep sigh of pure worry and frustration escaped her when she saw the soldiers go to Johann's place. Gerda slipped aside the curtain in the kitchen window. She peeked along the side, waiting to see the soldiers come outside again.

She could see Jodi and Anne's red toques bobbing up and down between the goal posts on the windmill yard where the kids were playing soccer.

It took the soldiers a long time to search Johann Mulder's home—or so it seemed. Gerda breathed a deep sigh of relief when she saw the soldiers leave empty-handed.

Gerda turned around to look at the clock that hung on the kitchen wall. It was five o'clock in the afternoon. Almost suppertime. Her legs felt rubbery all of a sudden. She tried to force a little smile on her face before she sank down on a kitchen chair.

The weary mother folded her small, veined hands on the tabletop and bent over praying, trembling inside. Gerda acutely felt the harsh reality of her own problems overwhelming her, more so now than ever before.

Oh, if only Derk were home. Gerda felt as if she were living in a dark room, looking for a door out. She groaned softly.

7

Hunger

It had been a sultry, snowy day, which was unusual for this time of year. Just enough snow had fallen to transform the small Dutch village of Nyverdal into a charming, pure white wintery village scene.

It was October 1944.

Gerda slumped over the kitchen chair, stroking her tired forehead.

Hopeless, she fought back the tears stinging the back of her eyes. Each day, she and her family gave thanks to the Lord for food and drink, but on this day there had been no food to thank Him for, so she had thanked Him for health and safety in general.

A cry escaped her heavy heart. *Alright, Lord, help us, please!* It was more a soul cry exploding from deep within than a demand. *How much longer can I cope with this uncertainty?*

Bert and Jodi had gone to bed crying with stomach cramps. Gerda knew they were caused by lack of food. Although the other children had not said a word, she could tell how hungry they were by the hollow look in their eyes as they'd gone to bed. Where could she find food to feed her starving family? Gerda held back the tears welling up in her eyes

Gerda had heard that the government was to set up a food voucher program soon, but nothing had materialized so far. Desperation stamped her face. *Where can I find food, any kind of food?* Gerda, the woman who always managed to portray a friendly smile, tried to identify the churning emotions that took hold of her.

Gerda got up from her chair and walked over to the kitchen cupboard, where she pulled open the bottom door. She knelt down, knowing the top shelves were completely empty. Gerda bent her head until it was touching the floor. She tried to look at the very end of the shelf to find the least bit of food anywhere! It was empty, too. Gerda placed her right hand way down underneath. She made a sweeping motion, praying to find some evidence of edible food, anywhere! She found nothing. Not even a tiny breadcrumb.

She worked herself back up from her crouching position and walked over to the kitchen table again. The thin lines in her forehead deepened every step of the way. Her eyes were burning from lack of sleep. She fell on a chair, clumsily.

The eyes that used to glisten with joy now swam with tears. The small veined hands that had been wrung, blistered, pinched, and bitten throughout the years lay quietly folded on the table. The dead-tired, weary mother of ten bent her head down low. From the very bottom of her heart came a soft cry: "Heavenly Father, surely you know the worries I have for my family. Lord, I beg of You, help us, please!"

Gerda lifted her head. She looked into space as if she'd seen a clear vision. She bent her head once again. "But, Lord, You promised to take care of Your children… I know You will!" Her tortured eyes demonstrated that she was under a great deal of stress.

She suddenly squared her shoulders. Her voice sound crisp and clear now as she recalled out loud the words Derk had read from the Bible at the supper table the last time he'd been home some eight weeks ago: *"The Lord is my helper; I will not be afraid"* (Hebrews 13:6).

Gerda stood up and, with a firm expression on her face, shoved her chair away from the table. She wiped away the tears with the slip of her apron, then walked to the living room and looked out the window. The light outside had disappeared long since. The stars were beginning to show off their miraculous beauty in the frosty sky.

She suddenly heard the sound of rushed, booted footsteps. She peeked behind the window curtain and saw a shadow slip by the window. Gerda cast an anxious look. An icy chill touched the back of her neck. Next, there came a rushing knock. Before she could answer it, the door opened and a heavy, dark-haired man with a kind face came inside. The man looked to be in his early sixties. He dug his hands in his big overcoat pockets and extracted a loaf of bread from one pocket and a pound of butter, wrapped in heavy paper, from the other.

The messenger cleared his throat a few times, as if he were trying to find the right words to say. He had a concerned look in his dark grey eyes. "Derk told me to bring this to you," he said. He turned around, walked to his bicycle, and opened a big black suitcase. He grunted as he took hold of a twenty-five pound sack of grain. "Sorry. I have no time to waste." He walked over to the kitchen counter and rested the sack on top. "The Germans think I am a doctor."

Next, he took the sack of grain and shoved it towards the back and out of sight. "Mrs. OpdenDries, you need to keep this out of sight," he emphasized as he let a smile reach his eyes. "The soldiers are getting hungry, too. Food is getting mighty hard to come by." He winked, then a mysterious weak smile lit up his face for the first time.

Gerda, still in a daze, said, "But, sir! Who… who are you?"

The gentleman put his hands on her shoulders. "Don't ask. Just call me Big John." But the look in Gerda's misty eyes changed his mind. "I am a friend of your husband's. I work for the Dutch government. Derk is a good man, Mrs. OpdenDries, a good man. Your husband keeps working hard in the underground whenever he is able. He helps the Resistance Movement nearly every day." The man looked up at the clock. "I've got to get going, now!" He walked to the door, then turned. "Derk said for you not to worry about food."

"But... but where are Derk and the boys staying?" Gerda clasped her hands anxiously in front of her.

Big John hesitated momentarily. His dark eyes mirrored sadness. "All I can tell you is that we have to move them from one place to the other occasionally. How and where, I cannot tell you. You cannot tell the fanatic S.S. soldiers what you don't know, right? You know what I mean?" A sheepish grin spread across his face. Before turning to leave, he dug his hand into his inside pocket once more. "Here's a couple of food rationing tickets Derk saved for you. The government has promised to start distributing rationing tickets very soon now." With that, Big John disappeared with a wave of the hand. "I'll be coming by every now and then to bring food for your family. Trust me."

Before Big John hit the road on his bicycle, Gerda slumped down by the table once more. This time it was a move fostered by the jubilant song of thanksgiving in her heart. Gerda lifted her face with renewed hope towards heaven.

"I thank You, Lord, for the food and good news about Derk and the boys. Thank You, Lord. They are alive!"

Gerda released pent-up tears of joy unafraid.

8

Bombings

The day dawned clear and cool with a blue sky. Though the sky was untroubled, the air was touched with the sweetness of budding springtime. The tender, lush green buds of the trees and the breath of lilacs and lilies generously shared their sweet fragrance all around.

At two o'clock that day, an English bomber squadron, with two Spitfire fighter planes escorting them, took to the air. Their destination: Nyverdal, Holland. It was early April 1945.

The sky was clear above the pilots heading for the coastal region in the centre of Holland. The large formation of aircraft looked like a large group of silver birds flying in perfect formation towards their goal. The rhythmic, steady drone of the engines encouraged pilots to stay alert.

The heavy-laden Lancaster bombers flew too low to be picked up by enemy radar control. Underneath the low flying aircraft glistened a deep and wide rippling blue ocean. Once the Dutch coast came into sight, the pilots told their gunners to take their positions.

The lively OpdenDries household suspected none of that. Shortly after the youngest children came home from school, they'd gone out in the neighbour's field to try flying a kite. Gerda quietly observed six airplanes skirting the town. She put her hand above her eyes and looked up into the sky. The noise of the airplanes set off a mournful little warning bell within her. A shiver run down her spine.

No, Lord, not again! We just had two bombings a few weeks earlier in this town.

Gerda noticed the first airplane take an abrupt dive, then the rest followed the same descent. She heard the loud whining of engines. The six airplanes released fire bombs, signalling bombing targets, then climbed back into the air, leaving buildings ablaze all around her.

I wonder if more planes will come?

Gerda quickly put both hands by her mouth and shouted to the children, who were playing on the grass across from her. "Come home, quick! All of you. Hurry! Go inside and take cover under the table, now!"

She heard another set of aircraft come their way, too. The living room window suddenly crashed in, and small pieces of metal came hurling through the broken windows. Gerda had no time to crawl under the table herself while the second wave of aircraft released splinter bombs, with deadly accuracy.

Gerda heard yet another, lighter kind of engine sound come roaring towards them. It was the English Spitfire fighters starting an air war with the German *Messerschmitt* fighter aircraft.

Gerda and her four children sat crouched under the table searching for cover from the falling debris that came through the open window.

"Mom, I'm so scared," Johan said, clinging to her in fear as fierce dogfights broke out and airplanes came tumbling down to earth.

The sky was ablaze with hammering noises. Scattering fragments hurled down from above.

Then came a ghostly silence. The boys crawled out from under the table and ran to the broken windows to look outside.

"Oh, look, Mom. Look! There's fire everywhere!" Sid shout. "Wow! Watch this airplane."

Everyone rushed to the window, where Sid stood watching a German fighter plane struggling to keep its balance, then burst into flames. A huge ball of fire remained stationary for a short moment, then the scarred *Messerschmit*, trailing a sheet of fire, plunged down to earth, splattering molten wreckage across a nearby farmer's field.

Awestruck, none of them noticed a third set of planes commissioned to produce another round of bombings over the town. They heard sudden screeching noises over the rooftop. Before anyone could take cover, there was a blinding explosion close by. Debris came through the broken window once again. Dust swirled around in the house, followed by a high-pitched whizzing noise. They heard fragments of bombs hit against the bricks outside their home.

Everyone automatically shielded their eyes from the bright glare. "A bomb must have landed close by," Gerda muttered softly, more to herself then to any member of her family. At long last, she uncovered her eyes. "Stay put, all of you, just in case there's another attack coming."

Gerda looked on as if in a dream. There was debris and glass scattered all around her. Smoke came in through the open windows. She got up and walked over to the shattered living room window.

Oh, no! Look at the huge fire!

Gerda's youngest brother Henk's house on the end of Mill Street had been bombed. It was engulfed in an all-out blaze of fire! Gerda started looking around. She saw nothing but bombed-out buildings on fire, heaved-up pavement, and debris strewn all over the road.

The awful consequences slowly began to dawn on her bewildered mind. Gerda gripped the windowsill to keep her balance momentarily, then turned away from the window and wobbled towards the kitchen. She sank beside her paralysed, dejected children, who were clinging to each other under the kitchen table. Gerda told them to come out from under the table. She placed her protective arms around them.

"What about Bert and Jodi, Mom?" Johan's voice was shaky. "Thursday is the day they have to go to school in the country, remember?"

Gerda, acutely aware of the tense and fearful situation, gathered her children all around like a mother duck gathers her chicks.

"Come," she said. "We must pray that the Lord above helps us out."

Gerda slowly looked around the damaged room as though it was for the first time. Only the strain in her eyes and a faint twitching of her upper cheek betrayed her inner struggle with the fearful situation they were in. An unusually eerie silence blanketed the war-torn room.

It seemed like an eternity before Gerda directed a solemn gaze towards the heavens. Gerda placed her arms tightly around the fearful children. "Dear Lord up above, please be with little Jodi and Bert. I beg of You, please bring both home safely, and… and Lord, be with Derk and the boys. Keep all of us safe in Thy tender care, I beg of You." Then the seemingly always strong Gerda OpdenDries broke down in a torrent of tears, still huddling her fearful children.

Sudden voices down the street brought her back to reality.

"Let's all go look out the window," she said. They stepped over the pieces of glass strewn across the floor and huddled by the broken living room window, a picture of pure hopelessness. Gerda and her young ones longingly looked down Mill Street, hoping to see Bert and Jodi come home. All they could see were houses left in smoking rubble, smoke-filled air, and streets filled with scorched bricks, glass, wood, and innocent, twisted bodies. Gerda looked down the horizon and saw small tufts of picturesque clouds against the glare of the burning fires all around.

Depressed beyond words, Gerda's mind was numbed with shock. "If only Derk were home," she said softly so no one would hear.

"Mom, can Dick and I go out to collect strips of aluminum and bullet shells?" Sid asked. He puffed up his chest to look more mature. "Please, Mom? I want to collect them to trade with my friends at school tomorrow."

Gerda saw Sid's innocent blue eyes staring with excitement into a cruel world he did not yet understand. *Oh, the bliss of innocence.* Gerda sighed. "No, Sid. Not at this time just yet."

She looked up to see what time it was. The clock had stopped at 3:15 in the afternoon.

Gerda walked over to look out the broken window to see if she could find Bert and Jodi coming down the street. She felt cold and tired, dead tired, as she walked over to the big easy chair in the living room. Gerda dropped into it and let a flood of tears blind her.

Crying is all I do lately, she thought.

"Lord, why?" Her voice broke. She buried her face in her hands. A flood of tears fell from her eyelashes, blinding her once more. Her lips moved, but no sound came out.

She was praying for her husband Derk, all of her children, and the whole wide world.

That day, the finger of death stretched out to claimed yet another 72 lives in Nyverdal. More than three hundred twisted wounded lay among the dead scattered in the streets.

9

Where's Mom?

"Bert, I'm so afraid!" Jodi sobbed. With the back of her small hands, she tried to wipe away the tears trickling down in a straight line on her round face.

Bert turned around. He put his arm around her shoulder and whispered in her ear, "Come, Jodi, we'll find Mom and the rest real soon now." Tugging her along, Bert squeezed her hand tightly to show her how much he cared.

Eleven-year-old Bert and nine-year-old Jodi were on their way home from school. Ever since their own school had been bombed over half a year ago, the two had attended classes in a large farmhouse a good twenty-minute walk from home, every Thursday, once a week.

Bert usually enjoyed taking this long walk out in the countryside, but today was different. There seemed to be an awful lot of townspeople heading for the country. Some people were crying. When Bert and Jodi got closer to town, they saw people coming towards them, bleeding from cuts and bruises on their hands and faces.

Jodi stopped again. She looked as if she was going to begin weeping. The corner of her mouth began to twitch. Her mouth tightened. She stood biting her lip. "I don't want to go home, Bert." She pointed her finger in the direction of Nyverdal. "See, there's a lot of dark smoke in town. Something happened. I'm so afraid something happened to Mom."

Bert looked puzzled and his eyes widened. Bert gently put his arms around his little sister, his face radiant with affection. "No matter what, Jodi, we've got to find Mom. She may need me." He nearly shout at her in frustration. Bert grabbed her by the hand. "Come along, hurry!" He forcefully started pulling Jodi's arm. Fighting back his own tears, he yelled, "Let's go, Jodi! Now!"

But Jodi refused. He looked around in desperation, then saw a middle-aged man coming towards them.

The man tapped Bert on the shoulder. "Don't go any further," he said, nodding his head in the direction of the town. "It's been pretty rough going out there." He took Bert's hand. "Let's go inside my farmhouse till things settle down in Nyverdal. That's better for you."

The farmer took Bert and Jodi to an open area in his cattle barn. The barn was filled with people. Some were excited, talking loudly. Others were crying.

Bert saw two children crying, with bleeding legs and cut faces. He shivered. Jodi pulled her hand back again. "I don't want to stay in this strange place," she said.

"Here's a place for you to sit down," the farmer said. "I will get a drink for you two."

Bert put his arms around Jodi's shoulder again. It dawned on him suddenly that he had heard a few airplanes circling above the town. Had there been a bombing in town?

The kind farmer had the good intention of bringing them a glass of water, but more and more wounded came inside his barn who needed help first. Bert made a grown-up decision. He quickly calculated the situation and jumped to his feet. "Come along, Jodi. Let's go find Mom, quick!" Bert pulled her along outside.

The two scurried out of the wide open barn doors and started running down the road towards home.

Ten minutes later, Bert and Jodi came around the corner of Mill Street, where they lived. There was smoke everywhere. Bert saw their house in the middle of the block. His face lit up. "Our house is still standing, Jodi. It was not bombed!"

Bert then looked in the other direction, where he saw Uncle Henk's bicycle store, four houses away, in a heap of rubble. It was still smouldering. Bert and Jodi hopped over scorched bricks and bomb fragments trying to get home.

Soldiers and ambulance attendants were busy looking after dead and wounded lying in the streets, but they paid no attention to either of the children. Once Bert and Jodi came past the windmill yard, they saw ambulance drivers put Theo, the mill owner's son, on a stretcher. Theo screamed in anguish and pain. Bert saw a sharp bomb fragment sticking out of his friend's right leg. Bert started wiping his own eyes when he saw that his best friend was covered in blood.

Jodi stopped again. "I can't go on, Bert. I feel sick to my stomach!"

Nudging her shoulder, Bert said, "Come, Jodi, our house is right there. I know Mom is there! She's waiting for us right now." He tried to sound reassuring, but deep down he was not even sure their mom was still alive.

Stepping between scattered bricks, glass, and sand, the two reached their partially ruined home. Bert peeked through the living room window to see if he could see their mom.

Their big sister Hennie was the first to see them. "Mom!" she screamed. "Bert and Jodi are home!"

Bert and Jodi could hear their mom cry out in loud voice, "Bert! Jodi! You've come home!"

Jodi let go of her pent-up tears. "Mom!" she cried out.

Gerda ran towards them with open arms, uttering shouts of pure happiness. The trio jumped for joy amongst the scorched rubble and ruins.

"Come, let's go inside and sit down for a while," Gerda said with a cheerful voice. Although she'd been terribly upset with the recent bombings, at this moment her face lit up. It was not an ordinary joy, but genuine thankfulness that all her younger children had been saved by the almighty Hand of God.

Gerda watched silently as her children comforted each other with loving concern, ignorant of the havoc created by the unwanted bombings that day.

Sid, with carpentry on his mind, stood observing the broken windows and cracked walls. “Are we going to stay in this house, Mom?”

Before Gerda had a chance to answer, one of the older boys, Marcel, took the lead. “I think not, Sid,” he said. “We should go stay with Mom and Dad’s friends in Den Ham. It’s only twenty kilometres down the road. I think we best get packing our stuff, Mom!” Marcel sounded firm and sure of his actions, convinced Gerda needed him at this particular point in time.

“Isn’t there a place closer where we can stay, Mom?” Sid asked.

Gerda sighed. “Our neighbour, Theo Aaltink, stopped by to tell us that we could stay with his parents until the house gets fixed.” Her voice sound drained, as if she did not know how to tackle the move without her husband, Derk.

“Is that the place where they make wooden shoes, Mom?” Sid replied.

“Sure is!” Marcel tapped his younger brother on the shoulder. “Maybe you and I can learn how to make wooden shoes out of a tree. Wouldn’t that be fun?” Marcel took a sideways glance at Gerda. “We best try to get there before dark, don’t you think, Mom?”

Hennie and the others had already packed a few things to take along.

"I wish Derk and the older ones were here to help," Gerda said.

But she had no time to wonder. Two neighbours soon came along with a team of horses and a wagon. The driver shook hands with Gerda. "We must get going to get there before dark, Mrs. OpdenDries," he spoke with a rushed tone in his voice.

Gerda regained her composure. She was relieved that she would not have worry about how to move her family to a safe place anymore.

All are safe, at least. It could have been so much worse.

Gerda bowed her head momentarily. She whispered a quick silent prayer amongst the hustle to get going to Den Ham, a much safer place to live.

10

Freedom at Last

It was a warm, sunny day. The sun stood high in a crystal blue sky. A few sheep-like clouds moved about as if they were playing a game of catch-up.

Gerda stared out the living room window onto the sun-drenched street, her hands clenched in front of her. Deep lines of worry and exhaustion etched in her tired face revealed the harsh time of suffering and despair she'd experienced these last five years.

There lay an eloquent story of pain in the cautious movement of her quivering lips when she began to pray softly. The very thought of freedom from oppression, and Derk and the boys coming home to stay, rekindled new life in this gutsy little woman.

It was 12:15 p.m., May 5, 1945.

Gerda abruptly stopped her musings at the sound of running feet. Ten-year-old Jodi came racing into the kitchen's back door, panting for breath. She came to a screeching halt in front of Gerda, her cheeks flushed from running and her eyes shining like a star.

"There's... there's great big machines rolling down the street, Mom!" Jodi grabbed hold of Gerda's hand. "Come along, Mom. Hurry!" In her excitement, Jodi did not notice her mom's misty eyes. "There's... there's soldiers on top of the big machines, Mom, and... and they are not German soldiers. Never seen this kind before. Come quick!" Jodi paused to swallow. "These soldiers are smiling at us. Smiling, Mom! Let's go, hurry!"

Gerda called upstairs to Hennie, "Come along, Hennie!"

Hennie came hustling down the narrow stairway. "Hurry, Mom. Something is happening out there. I saw it through the window upstairs. Let's get going!"

Hennie rushed ahead of Gerda. Jodi was way down the street already. At the end of the driveway, Gerda and Hennie heard strange noises from heavy tanks and motorcycles. Gerda quickly shaded her eyes in an attempt to determine what direction the noises were coming from.

Jodi soon come back to tug Gerda along, "Come on, Mom, hurry!" she said. "Marcel and the others are waiting for us at Main Street. Hurry! Come on now!" Jodi lost patience with Gerda's slower pace.

Gerda had been praying all along that the war would be over soon. She had read in the newspaper the night before that German troops, dug in all around town, had been flushed out by Canadian soldiers earlier that day. All night long, she'd heard fighting going on in the outskirts of town, but Gerda, like everyone else, did not dare shout for joy just yet. What if the enemy came back with a final spurt of deadly violence against them?

Gerda had a hard time convincing her sons to stay at home with soldiers so close by fighting the enemy. But once the sporadic gunfire went quiet, there was no holding them back. The whole town was dancing in the streets, in an uproar.

When Gerda and Jodi got to the end of Mill Street, Jodi let go of her mom's hand. She wiggled her way through cheering crowds lined three deep all along Main Street.

A smile slid across Gerda's face as she watched her little girl try ducking under the waving arms of others, bound and determined to join her friends waving to these friendly soldiers. They were called "Liberators"! A tall, heavy-set man looked at Jodi trying to get through to the front of the line. He smiled and moved sideways to let her go by.

Gerda, caught up in the excitement, started waving and cheering at the Canadian soldiers sitting on their tanks with artillery machines rolling by. "Thank you, soldiers. Thank you for freedom... thank you all!" Everyone was screaming loudly and waving Dutch flags.

Gerda felt warm tears running down her cheeks. She was not ashamed in the least! In her own excitement, Gerda had lost track of Jodi. By shifting around and craning her neck, she was able to see her daughter's big white hair ribbon bouncing up and down wildly up ahead. Her wooden shoes made loud rhythmic sounds on the pavement as she waved, jumped, and screamed right along with the rest of them.

Jodi paused momentarily. She saw a soldier dig his hands into his pockets and throw two big chocolate bars her way. She leaped forward. Jodi figured at least a hundred hands were reaching for the same chocolate bar.

But no. One landed straight in her hands! She turned around. "Mom, see!" She could not find Gerda, so she slipped the bar into her pocket. "I'll share it tonight, Mom," she whispered. "Don't worry."

Gerda's spirits were lifted high. The jubilant crowd swept away the cares and worries she had experienced earlier that morning.

Hennie kept looking around to see if she could find her boyfriend Henk Wever in the crowd. Just then, she heard the sound of her name being called. She saw Henk waving his arm, calling for her. Hennie turned to find Gerda. "I've got to go see Henk, Mom. Don't worry about me. I'll come home soon." And off she went.

Gerda felt a sudden nudge, as if by an unseen hand. Her heart quickened its pace. She pulled away from the cheering crowd to look down Mill Street. She had to shade her eyes against the bright sunshine. Then, she saw four figures coming down the road towards her.

"It's Derk and the boys!" she howled.

Nothing but her family mattered at that moment. Without delay, Gerda roughed her small figure under the arms of waving bystanders until she caught sight of Jodi. Her other boys were all over the place.

Gerda grabbed her youngest daughter's outstretched hand and shouted, "Jodi, Dad and the boys are home! Hurry! Let's go meet them, quick!" Gerda pulled Jodi along. Squeezing her hand tightly, the two ran blindly down Mill Street.

"It's Dad and the boys! I see them, Mom, see?" Jodi shouted, looking up to her.

Derk and the boys came running towards them. Josh scooped up Jodi in one sweeping motion.

"Oh, how I missed all of you," Josh said, kissing her red cheeks. "I love you!"

Derk's voice sounded hysterical. Embracing Gerda, he shouted in her ear, "My darling, we're home to stay!"

Josh, Martin, and Tom took turns hugging Gerda and their little sister. They all started dancing for joy in the middle of the street, but no one cared. They were free from tyranny! Free at last!

Derk whispered in Gerda's ear, "Maybe, just maybe, I will see my lifelong dream come true of immigrating our family to a country called Canada, the land of promise."

"Let's not think about that right now, Derk," Gerda replied. "Today is a time of joy for everyone. A time of freedom, Derk!" She looked towards the heavens with unwavering, steady eyes.

"Where's the rest of the family, Mom?" asked Josh.

"Oh, somewhere out there!" Gerda answered, joy kindling her eyes like a bright twinkling star. Her face revealed the dawning of relief from war and tyranny.

Derk, Gerda, and their children hustled their way home through the cheering, dancing crowds that surrounded them.

Later that night, Derk thought of the huge advertising billboard he'd seen by the main road before the war broke out. There was a gorgeous picture of a clean, new place that looked like a modern Eden. It was of a field of wheat, and in front of it was a happy farmer and his wife with a baby in her arms and kids playing in the yard. *"Welcome to Alberta, Canada,"* it had read.

"Gerda, I'm going to see tomorrow if we can immigrate our family to Canada," Derk said, brimming with enthusiasm for the newborn hope inside of him.

Derk, having lost forty pounds during the last few years, could feel the excitement of adventure regain entry in his thoughts. He had a vision of his family living in a new country, delighting in working the job of their choice, and enjoying horseback riding like Western cowboys on the wide open prairies of Alberta, Canada, where his sister Mina and her husband were already farming.

Maybe my dream will soon become a reality after all.

Derk's eyes twinkled in anticipation of a better future.

11

Farewell Fatherland

The sky was a wide, pristine blue. There was a soft whispering wind and a kind of blistering, brazen warm sunshine most unusual for that time of year.

Twenty-five-year-old Josh OpdenDries stood in the scorching sun by the passenger side of a small bus, helping his family step down on the paved ship-docking yard. Josh gave Jodi an extra little hug. She wiggled out of his arms to go stand by the rest of the family. They were watching a long line of cargo ships lulling peacefully in the harbour of Rotterdam, Holland.

The docks were alive with activity. Crews were hauling flour barrels, grain bags, salted beef, boxes of bread, and sacks of carrots, turnips, and potatoes. Trolleys backed up onto the loading ramps, loaded with provisions. They clattered empty back to the warehouse for more supplies, enough to last the 845 passengers on the former troop ship known as *Kota Inten.* It would be a ten-day journey across the ocean.

It was April 8, 1948.

It took the OpdenDries boys and Hennie's boyfriend Henk, who had decided to immigrate to Canada with the Dries family, only ten minutes to fill their eyes with the huge oceanliner, swaying back and forth in the water.

"Come!" yelled Henk. "Let's go have a look by the ocean!"

The boys took off.

"Come back here, all of you!" Derk's deep voice thundered over the water. "We need to check in our passports at the immigration office."

Johan rolled his eyes. "But Dad, those are the biggest ships in all the world! Don't you see?"

Derk tapped him on the shoulder. "You'll be on one of those ships for a whole ten days, my boy."

"But Dad," Bert said, near to bursting out in tears, "there's a whole line of people going up that plank into the ship. We don't want to be late, do we?"

Derk glanced at his watch. "The ship won't leave for another two hours." He bent down and picked up two heavy suitcases. "Follow me. All of you!"

Little Jodi could not imagine, even from picture books, that ships could be so large. "Look at all those people on the boat, Dad." She waved her arms, motioning towards the top deck where bunches of people were gathering.

"Don't you worry," Gerda said. "We'll be going up there soon,"

The whole family kept marching towards the immigration offices inside the station.

Josh and his wife Dina had decided to stay behind in Holland to take care of Dina's mother. Her father was one of the many people who had died in the last bombing attacks in Nyverdal, a few years before.

Josh and Dina walked with the family towards the ocean liner, which was patiently waiting to load Dutch immigrants destined for Canada. Dina watched and listened to the soft moaning from a listless breeze coming in from the east. She enjoyed the wind, which caused the lulling waves to gently lap against the ship's bow. But Josh saw none of that. His searching eyes were raised upwards to where huge smokestacks threw thick ringlets of dark smoke up into the sky.

Josh counted the lifeboats fastened alongside the ship right above the passenger island in the midsection. A worried look shadowed his face.

Dina took his hand. "What's worrying you, Josh?"

"Oh, nothing," he said, trying to act nonchalant. "It's just that I know the *Kota Inten* is nothing but an old troop ship used in the war. I know it's seen a lot of action. I just wonder how good it will be in a heavy storm at sea."

"So? What can you do about that?"

"I wonder if this ship had a proper overhaul after the war," Josh spoke absentmindedly.

She slapped him on the shoulder. "Oh, you goof!" She threw a teasing look in his direction. "Come, let's go have a look at your excited family, shall we?"

They saw Bert come running towards them. "Dad says we are ready to roll!" The boy's eyes glistened with joy. The rest of the family followed behind him, tugging along heavy suitcases.

"I guess it's time to say goodbye to you all," Josh said, trying to hide the deep hurt he felt inside over having to part with his family. *Will I ever see any of them again?* Josh pinched his little brother Bert's nose. "You be sure to write me about the wild, wild Western cowboys, you hear?" Josh made a quick turnaround, as if trying to forget his loss.

Gerda threw both her arms around Josh. Pressing his face against hers, she cried, "We'll miss you so much, Josh. Be good to Dina, promise?" She then hugged Dina, who knew so well what it was like to miss somebody you loved. Would they ever meet again?

Derk stood aside, watching the whole scenario with sensitive eyes. He came up the Josh, and took him by the hand. Derk then looked into the round, deep blue eyes of his oldest son.

"I've been mighty proud of you, Josh." Derk swallowed. "My thanks for all the work you have done for the family, especially in the war years. Remember…" Derk pointed towards heaven. "Our heavenly Father will be looking after all our affairs, both here and in Canada." He gave his son a firm slap on the shoulder.

Derk looked at Gerda sideways. "Come, Gerda, we've got nine others to take care of. Let's get going."

Josh and Dina waited on the dock. They watched the ship turn without much effort, heading towards open seas. They waited until they could see the ship no more.

Josh sighed. "We best be going home, Dina. Our home." He squeezed her arm.

Once the *Kota Inten* hit the calm open seas, she seemed to pass effortlessly over the waves without much effort, adjusting herself to the irregularities in the water like an otter in a fast stream.

The ship's captain milled about amongst the passengers on deck. He put a handheld loudspeaker to his mouth. "Attention, please!" The captain's voice boomed loud and clear. "The ship's crew and captain wish you a pleasant journey to your new homeland. Ship's crew members shall direct you to your living and dining room areas aboard the ship. All female passengers will have their sleeping quarters in the ship's stern down below. Men's lodging is located at the back of the ship below deck. This is your captain speaking."

Sleep did not come easy to Gerda, Hennie, and Jodi that first night. They had been assigned to a row of hang mats amongst hundreds of hammocks swaying to and fro with the ship's lulling movements.

Jodi lay on the bottom mat. She peeked her eyes open periodically to a set of hang mats across the aisle. There was an awfully heavy lady there with plenty of "cushioning."

Some of the other passengers called her "Aunt Josi." She lay in the bottom hammock. Her hang mat did not sway nearly as much as the rest of them, but Jodi was dreadfully scared that, in a storm, Aunt Josi's low-hanging buttocks could easily come crashing down on the wooden floor straight beneath her.

A good hour later, Jodi fell asleep, dreaming of huge waves and a screaming Aunt Josi.

When they awoke the next morning, they detected a sweet, smoky breeze from the southeast. The waves were small and weak, as though they lacked the strength to ever rise again. The tame ocean looked like a ruffled, endless sheet of soft velvet.

Ten days later, on April 18, the new immigrants stepped on the ship's unloading plank in Halifax, Nova Scotia, to bring them to the shores of their new homeland, Canada.

Gerda felt quiet and reserved. Her lips parted a little once they hit solid ground. She looked around amongst the milling crowd. *A new country… where will this lead to?* She bit her lip to keep tears from spilling down her cheeks. She hoped Derk and the children would not notice. But of course, Derk did.

Although surrounded by her family, amongst a shouting, shoving group of new immigrants, Gerda felt alone. Emptiness filled her heart that she could not have put into words.

Derk sensed her emotional upheaval. He lifted her chin gently, his face alight with tenderness and care. "Gerda, together we've come through hard wartimes. We're going to need to face the future in a strange new homeland with a positive attitude. Shall we, please?"

As he looked into her eyes, a new hope stirred down deep inside of him. He firmly believed in the bright future ahead for all his family.

Shoulders drooped, Gerda smiled. But it was a twisted smile as tears started tickling the back of her eyes. She swallowed the biggest lump she'd ever known. She looked at Derk with misty eyes and saw new hope beaming in his face.

She raised herself up with dignity, wiped her eyes, and proceeded to overlook the hustling, scrambling crowd that surrounded her. Solemn resolve and pride welled up in her as she regained her self-control and former elegance.

Although Gerda portrayed no particular emotion other than a straightening of her drooping figure, she stood like a sergeant major, with straight, squared shoulders. She started tapping her right foot, a gesture she'd been known to perform whenever she reached a clear-cut decision. She decided that no matter what problems lay ahead of her, she would try to adopt a cheerful attitude for Derk's sake and the sake of her family.

Nonetheless, in the depth of her soul there hankered a belief that she had left something very dear to her behind—her son Josh. Would she ever see him again?

12

Along Dusty Trails

After a four-day trip on the train from Halifax to Lethbridge, Alberta, the OpdenDries family arrived on April 22, 1948, at the home of Derk's sister Mina and her husband Cris Wirda. The Wirdas lived in the small town of Monarch, to the northwest of Lethbridge.

Mina was a bird-like woman, small, neat and tidy, with dark eyes set in a kind, round face. Her eyes seemed ready to burst into laughter at any moment. Her sparkling expression foreshadowed the special kind of elegance and good will she shared with anyone she took a liking to.

Her husband Cris was a jolly, slim-faced man with brilliant blue eyes and a dazzling smile. He was not overly tall and a bit heavy, but he didn't stick out in any particular area; he was just stocky, broad and solid everywhere. His ruddy face could have been the face of a much younger man but for the swathes of silver in the slightly greying hair above it.

Cris told Derk that his family was welcome to stay at their place for one week—just to get a handle on things.

Mina, Cris, and their son Henry spent most of the week showing the OpdenDries family what life was like in their new country. Mina cautiously warned Gerda over a cup of coffee about the raw living conditions they might find at their new place in the town of Picture Butte, where they were headed.

"I think you should prepare yourselves to go back in history about twenty years or so," she told Gerda. "There will be no electricity, running water, or a bathroom inside the house. There never is in these kinds of homes."

"How will I do the washing and cook food and all that?" Gerda asked. She had visions of big piles of laundry stacked up around the house.

"In the summer, most people use irrigation water from the ditches. Winter is much better, Gerda. You can use melted snow water to do the wash. If you hang the clothes outside to dry on a clothesline, they harden like icicles. But if you're lucky with a bit of wind, the clothes will be half-dry by evening."

Monday morning, after a one-week stay with Cris and Mina, both families were seated around the breakfast table. Bright early morning rays of sunlight shone a playful, yellow-orange tint over the items on the table.

Cris fervently twisted the points of his thick, handlebar moustache, then squinted at Derk. The lines around his tiny, pebble-like eyes deepened.

"After one week of loafing around, Derk, I say we'd best get a move on to Picture Butte," Cris said. His fingers extracted a rusty round watch from the pocket of his striped coverall. He brought the watch close to his face. "I think it's just about time for you all to relocate to your new place in sugar beet country up yonder, Derk."

"I've been wondering about the trip, Cris," said Derk, dressed in a checkered cotton shirt and blue jeans. "How many hours will it take for us to get there?"

"I think we's could be there in about an hour's drive, depending on road conditions this time of year," Cris said. His eyes twinkled as a sly grin slid across his face.

Cris and Mina were what folks called early pioneer settlers that had come to the rugged Wild West frontier in southern Alberta before the Second World War.

A couple of days before the OpdenDries family arrived, Cris and his son Henry had been busy scraping up enough wood from around the yard to build tall stock racks on Cris' 1932 three-ton Ford truck, his pride and glory.

"It sure isn't for nothing them young whippersnapper friends of yours is just a mite jealous of this fine motorized contraption, son," Cris told Henry. He let his right hand wander softly across the shiny yet rusty fender as if it were a newborn child. He took a few steps backwards, a smile of satisfaction framing his face. "Yep, she's a mighty slick looking vehicle."

Henry nodded. "Yep, she's a fine looking vehicle, son. Fine looking, indeed."

Cris slipped the left hand into the crux of the right arm. He cupped his right hand and manoeuvred his chin to rest comfortably in this position. He cast a sideways glance in his son's direction.

After breakfast, Cris and Derk proceeded to take an easy stroll down the narrow lane that led towards a shed where Cris kept his Ford truck and the bright red 1930 Model-A family car.

Derk inhaled deeply of the fresh country air. Derk looked at the slightly taller Cris beside him. "Oh, doesn't it feel good to breathe in this fresh wide open country air, Cris?"

"Yep, Derk. I love this country. Pure, bright, and peaceful living here in Canada."

As they passed Mina's carefully tendered rockery, the path widened into a huge strip of lawn that led all around the house. Derk took note of the dead yellow grasses. They looked unkempt, but the detailed trellises and flowerbeds lent visions of pretty flowers and climbing wisteria forcing their tendrils all along the south side of the house. Right along the budding flowerbeds were an untidy variety of hardy perennials locked in a dire battle with a jungle of dead weeds trying to push their new young shoots about in every direction.

Cris made a sudden stop, then thrust both hands into the side pockets of his striped coveralls. He gazed upwards, straining his eyes. There was not a cloud in sight to disturb the matchless deep blue sky above. He felt the warm sunshine on his back and felt that funny kind of feeling creep inside him that pioneering folk called "a spring fever attack."

Cris made his way up to the shed. He walked around the Ford truck and inspected it with a touch of fear, as if he were afraid a few rats had been nibbling at it in his absence. He brought out a pink cloth and started polishing the fenders.

He glanced in Derk's direction. "Yep, Derk, we're ready to move along. We best get packing her today so we can make an early start tomorrow morning."

Derk looked up and down the rusty vintage truck with high wooden stock racks on both sides and a gateway in the back. The shed was crafted from uneven wood Cris and son Henry had found around the farmyard.

Derk walked around the truck for a final inspection. "Cris, do you think this truck will get us there?" he asked cautiously.

Cris quit polishing and turned slowly. He regarded Derk with hurt eyes. "Of course, man. This here shiny vehicle is one of the best four-wheeled wonders prancing around the country these days." Cris gave Derk a hard slap on his right shoulder. He looked at his barely roadworthy old jalopy with tender eyes. "Yep, Derk, sure thing! Sure thing! We'll get you and your family there safe and sound."

It had not taken Derk and Gerda long to figure out that their stay with Mina and Cris was a necessary training ground for them to learn some of the many different ways of life they'd have to get used to.

Mina had told Gerda and the girls a few tricks about cooking and housekeeping—a totally new way of what they were used to in their old country. Gerda and Hennie wrote down all sorts of information they'd need once they were moved into their own home.

Cris' announcement to get a move on to their own place, and meet the sugar beet farmer they'd all be working for, could not have come soon enough for Derk. Everyday he'd been thinking about building a brand new future for his family. The excitement inside of him grew deeper each passing day.

Derk let out a sigh of relief. *Finally, my dream will be fulfilled.* "I'll be getting my boys to help us pack, Cris." He turned so that he didn't waste another minute just standing there looking around in idleness.

Cris, Derk, and the older boys spent most the day packing and loading the provisions they'd need to help them make do three miles away from the nearest town, Picture Butte.

Gerda was ever so grateful for the church people and neighbours who had given them enough bedding, clothes, cooking utensils, and furniture to help them last until the end of June, when their own goods would arrive by boat from Holland in two big wooden crates.

Early on April 23, when the clock struck eight o'clock in the morning, Cris opened the garage door and looked at the truck loaded to the brim. Pots and pans even hung on the outside of the stock racks.

Gerda, Hennie, and Jodi jumped into the Wirdas' family car. Cris' son Henry took to the steering wheel. Henry turned the key and started the car, then rolled down the driver side window. "Ready to go, Dad."

Cris turned the crank to start the truck motor. To his surprise, the engine coughed to life after only six turns of the crank. "Great working truck, Derk. Great stuff." Cris jumped behind the wheel and slowly drove the truck out of the garage. He parked near the front steps where seven excited OpdenDries boys were waiting to jump aboard.

Cris began to realize that there could be a few more problems than he'd bargained for. He stepped out of the truck and walked around it like an army sergeant. "Hold on now, boys. Let's just do some figuring on where to put you all!" He gently stroked the fingers of his right hand across his chin and threw a quick glance to where Henry was sitting behind the steering wheel in the car.

Gerda, Hennie, and Jodi sat like princesses in the car, grinning from ear to ear. Henry, too, had a broad grin on his young, good-looking face.

Cris, meanwhile, did some quick calculations in his head. "Four passengers in the truck cab and eight in the car makes twelve taken care of." Cris saw Derk trying hard to hold his boys back from jumping in the truck. "Well, well!

We'll be needing to pack an extra two young ones in the back of the truck!"

Hennie's boyfriend Henk stepped forward. "Hennie and I can sit in the back of the truck, Uncle Cris."

"Fine," Cris said. "Let's get them two settled first."

Henk was in the back already, having cleared a small place where the two could sit near the stock racks. It was tightly secured, since Cris had said it could be a bit of a rough ride down the road.

Cris grunt his approval and turned towards Derk. "You, Bert, and Jodi, come with me. The rest of you cramp in the car, you hear?" Cris turned to face his son. "By the way, Henry, you just keep on trucking right behind that good ol' truck of mine, you hear?" A broad smile wrinkled the corners of his lips.

"Don't worry, none, Pa." Henry tipped the brim of his hat and winked.

Cris filled his lungs with a deep breath of fresh, springtime air. He checked one last time to make sure everyone's seating arrangement was to their liking, then climbed behind the steering wheel of his favourite four-wheeled vehicle. "All aboard?" he yelled louder than necessary. "Let's get a move on!"

Cris set a heavy foot on the gas pedal. As the truck picked up speed, the pitch of the stuttering engine rose to a tortured scream. Rounding the bend at the end of the driveway to hit the main road, Cris waved a cheery farewell to his wife Mina. He tipped the rim of his hat slightly backwards, just enough so it would not fall off his head. He then steered the truck deftly between deep rutted grooves in the road, put there by heavy wagon wheels in what was called "spring break-up."

Once Cris hit the main road, he seemed to be in an even bigger rush to get moving.

Meanwhile, Gerda, who was sitting in the front seat of the car, looked out the side window and start waving goodbye to Mina, the small motherly type, who looked so happy with her lot in life.

Gerda felt a sudden loneliness creep over her. It almost felt as if she were paging through a picture storybook—the wild, empty garden and the tall, weathered pioneer home in front of which Mina had waved her farewell with a white handkerchief. Gerda shook her head. *I cannot comprehend how anyone can be so content living in such wild, God-forsaken country.*

Gerda's thoughts did not wander for long. Henry tried dodging big potholes in the road surface, hurtling the car at speeds up to forty kilometres an hour. Gerda tried to show neither fear nor her inner feelings by looking straight ahead out the window as she listened to the rhythmic thumping of the wheels and the occasional bumping back and forth. She recognized that travelling long distances over mud roads at this time of year was not for the faint of heart.

"Look," she said to her young ones. "See the lone boy horse, still in its winter coat? He's tossing his head and galloping in circles around the pasture, snorting in the springtime air."

Gerda tried spotting Cris' truck up a ways, but Cris merrily kept trucking along, leaving clouds of dust hurled up into the air by the narrow tires screeching back and forth between the numerous holes in the road. Gerda sat tight-lipped. She glanced to the back seat and saw her boys enjoying every minute of the bumpy ride with bright, glistening eyes.

Up ahead, Cris felt another rush of adrenaline take hold of him. He shoved his tall, striped hat up and turned down the window, looking around with a lively smile. He hummed loudly, as if he were sitting by the fireside in his ever so comfortable plush easy chair. He constantly fell off-key with grating, gurgling sounds that filled the cab when he hit the high-pitched notes.

Derk peered from underneath the brim of his cowboy hat. He hung onto Jodi, who was on his lap. Bert was squeezed in the middle, his round khaki-coloured cap hanging on to one side of his face. He bit his tongue, hanging onto the dashboard and bracing both feet against the floor boards.

The truck finally hit a long, straight patch of road. Derk gazed out the side window, seeing wide open prairie, dotted with grazing cattle, roll by in endless stretches. Here and there, he saw scattered homes with small farm yards between long swathes of windswept prairie land. Melting snow had already given way to yellow patches of last year's grassland and ploughed, dark brown earth. The grass had started turning green already. On the odd occasion, he could even make out a few pretty wild flowers blooming in ditches along the road. A flock of birds picked hastily over the leftover seeds in an unploughed field.

Derk looked at his watch. For a good sixty minutes, Cris had kept the vehicle between the ditches fairly well, though he continued his jolly whistling over the roar of the engine. Derk felt a headache coming on. He wound down the window. Maybe a sniff of fresh air would help him get rid of the headache. He hung his head out the window in search of relief to ease his edgy nerves.

He then looked back in the side mirror in time to see the outline of a car ghosting around the bend behind them in a trail of dust. *That must be Henry.*

A sudden gust of wind then peppered his face with the gritty spray of fine sands heaved up off the road. Derk quickly jerked his head inside and rolled up the window. He leaned forward. "How far till Picture Butte?" he bellowed, hoping to be heard above the roaring engine and Cris' singing.

Cris looked sideways and squinted his eyes into narrow slits. "With a bit of luck, we'll be there in about ten minutes."

His voice reached a high pitch that hurt Jodi's eardrums. She almost started to cry, but just as Cris' eyes left the road to look at Derk, the narrow wheels on the truck slipped into a deep mud track. Cris and all his passengers bounced around like a cork on wild waters. "Fear, not, Derk. We'll be just fine!" Cris managed to manhandle the truck to a steady ride with a few hasty left to right jerks on the steering wheel.

A car passed in the opposite direction. Cris moved his truck over as far as he could. "It's the thing to do, Derk. Sure thing, I say."

Cris dug in his pocket, produced a watt of snuff, and pushed it hard between his teeth towards one side of the mouth. Shading his eyes, Cris looked down the road. "Can't be too far anymore, Derk."

Another car passed. Cris made a jovial gesture with his arm to the man behind the wheel with a tattered cowboy hat and two screaming kids.

Bert, squashed between the two men, got the worst of the bumpy ride. The broad grin with which he had started this journey had changed to an occasional grimace of pain. When Bert saw that Cris had to tackle yet another turn at the bottom of a hill up ahead, he squeezed his eyes ever so tightly.

Cris had no fear. He let the truck speed faster and faster towards the bend in the road. Eventually, he tried to gear down, but the gears made awful noises. The truck continued faster down the hill at full speed. In response, Cris started doing what came natural—he jerked the wheel left to right so to break down the speed.

Grim-faced, Derk hung on to Jodi with one hand and the other hand on the doorknob.

Derk feared the end of his life was near. The thought struck him that the door he hung onto might easily fall off. If that happened, they'd all go tumbling out. Derk looked around for something else to hold onto for safety, but there was none.

Cris looked sideways and couldn't help but notice the fear stamped on the faces of his passengers. He started whistling: "She'll be coming round the mountain when she comes..."

Derk wound down the window once again in an attempt to let the fresh breeze run through his hair. *Oh, no!* He smelt a burning coming from underneath the hood. He pulled his head inside and cranked up the window fast and furious. He sensed he had all the symptoms of high blood pressure. Clenching his jaws, he felt his heart pounding irregularly.

He lifted his eyes towards the horizon, hoping for a sign of journey's end. There! Between a thin misty layer of dust, he saw a hazy outline of two lone houses on the far horizon.

Cris grunted loudly. "Yep! We're close now, Derk, real close!" he hollered. "Yep, I seen a big sign by the road that says 'Atkens Farm.' That's the place to be, Derk. Yes, sir, that's the place for you all." Cris reached over towards Bert and dug his bony fingers into the boy's shoulders. "Looks like we've come to the place of your destiny, my boy."

Derk let out a sigh of relief. *At long last!* Drops of perspiration flowed down the grooves of his forehead like a small river.

Cris grinded down the gears to slow down the vehicle. He muscled his truck around one last turn in the road and into a small narrow driveway. The truck stopped with a screeching of brakes a scant four feet away from the front doors of two empty, weather-beaten dwellings.

It was to be the OpdenDries' first home in the vast wide prairies of Alberta, Canada.

The family stepped out of the vehicles. Bright beams of sunshine glanced over the jumbled roofs of various shabby farm buildings spread about in a farmyard nearby.

The sky seemed endless, the air so much fresher. One could see for miles around. The measureless Canadian prairies held a special kind of unknown matchless beauty they could not have imagined.

13

Two Houses on the Lone Prairie

When Gerda and her children stepped out of the car, the sun bathed them with warm sunlight.

Gerda moved to stand in the warm midday wind with her usual touch of elegance. She looked meditatively, very erect with her head inclined and hands clasped in a tight fist in front of her. The heightened color in her face was evidence of her ruffled feelings. She let her eyes travel back and forth as she stared dumbfounded at the two neglected wooden homes, struck broadside by the full blaze of the early spring day. Her look wandered about the harsh, unkempt surroundings, so vastly different from what she had grown up with.

Her eyes were strained. There was hurt in them as she tried hard to get things into a proper perspective. She raised

her gaze up to the two chimney pipes fastened to the roof with barbed wire. A mixture of disbelief filled her inner being. The uneven roof was sagging, the back porch near falling down.

The two horribly neglected houses looked more like chicken coups than homes to live in.

Marcel came to stand beside her. "The foundations of these houses are as old as Methusalem, Mom," he mused.

It's almost like suddenly coming across a picture in an old book, Gerda thought. She moved a few steps closer to the second house a little farther down, not wanting the rest of the family see her bitter disappointment. Though usually mentally strong, she was thrown off-guard.

The day the OpdenDries family moved into their first home in Canada was April 29, 1948.

Derk came to stand beside Gerda. He put his arm around her shoulders, his eyes filled with concern. Gerda looked down, fighting back tears. He pulled her close to him, too stunned to think of anything positive to say.

"These houses are little more than old beaten shacks," he muttered softly.

His eyes wandered about. His mouth slightly open, Derk saw wooden steps made from timbers decayed a long time since. Tall tufts of old grass had grown in between the slats in front of the first shack. They had spread out, growing between the slats in the thirty-foot long wooden pathway separating both homes. The spindly grasses also stuck their heads up from beneath fallen fences all along the narrow road that led to the Picture Butte sugar beet factory, a few miles away.

Derk couldn't help but think of the nice, neat home they'd left behind in Holland, where there was not a blade of grass out of place, ever.

"Let's go have a look inside, Gerda," he said. He stepped on the wooden landing made from two-by-six planks that were crumbling around the outer edges. The landing wobbled under his weight. "Be careful, Gerda. It's a bit wobbly out here." Derk tried to grin, but his eyes mirrored grave discouragement.

He turned the doorknob and tried pushing the door open. After a second push, the door opened slowly. The hinges made groaning noises.

"Sounds like the hinges could stand a good oil job, Dad," Tom said.

Derk was astounded at what they saw. The inside of the house was smelly and dusty, with cobwebs everywhere. The floor was caked with mud from a former farmhand who'd lived there. It seemed like the house had not been lived in for a very long time, though. No ornaments of any kind hung on the walls.

Derk kicked a few mud pies caked on the floor. He walked over to the window, rubbed a bit of glass clean, and looked out. "There's a most marvellous view of Picture Butte Lake, right near our place." He tried not to sound sarcastic.

A lump formed in his throat. *How will Gerda and the girls adjust to these conditions? How will she accept such a forsaken mess and live in these houses? Can she?*

Gerda, Hennie, and Jodi walked around the shack. The uneven wooden floor was layered with sand that had blown in from outside. It looked as though someone had spilled a bag of sugar everywhere. Gerda studied the two small rooms for a while, then her eyes worked their way across the floors, the walls, and the crooked, hanging front door—the only door.

The kitchen had a wooden cook stove with an extra water basin to warm water in. A large barrel stood in the corner. "That's to keep boiled drinking water in," Cris explained.

It seemed like someone had brought in an apple crate table from the nuisance grounds downtown. There were no chairs to go along with it. "Guess one could call that rubbish," Gerda said, moving away. "Look at the cobwebs in the bedroom and everywhere else." She screwed up her nose. The house smelled like mice.

Hennie tried to open the small window above a ramshackle kitchen cupboard put together with rough lumber that could have been picked off the barn yard next door. The two shelves were held up by blocks of wood.

The window was stuck fast and the walls in both rooms were bare and plastered with whitewash.

Gerda walked into the bedroom. She saw old wallpaper, in a hideous pattern, peeled from the ceiling in more places than not. Gerda was taken aback, but had the good sense to put on a brave face. She stood on her toes, reached up, and took a dangling corner of the paper and tore it away from the wall. It fell on the floor in coils, bringing with it a cloud of mouldy plaster.

Gerda cleared her throat. "If we painted it white or cream colour, it might not look so bad." She tried to sound cheerful, but there was no happiness inside her.

She thought of the conveniences they had left behind in their old country—electricity, water, and their warm, nicely painted clean home. She walked over to the bedroom window and rubbed a bit of glass clean. She looked out on the wide open prairie. "It's certainly different from where we come from, right, Derk?" Her voice quivered. She snickered uncomfortably.

In the bedroom, there were two double beds with mattresses that sagged in the middle. A solid wooden wall separated them. Gerda cracked a smile. After a good five years of living under a brutal dictatorship, she had learned to perfect a certain toughness and philosophical attitude when it came to misfortunes that would have made most anyone else bang their heads against the wall. An optimist by nature, she had learned to shrug things off and say, "Oh, well, these things do happen. We'll work hard to overcome them. Better days will come to us someday."

Derk and the boys took a look outside. They saw a rusty old pump hung over a wobbly water trough.

"Oh, we can fix that, Dad," said Martin. "We'll do it tomorrow after work."

"How will you get to town to get new parts for the pump?" asked Marcel.

Martin shrugged. "We got a bicycle from Uncle Cris, remember?"

"But you don't even know how to speak English, Martin!"

"We learned some English in school, dummy. I know enough to tell them what we need. Besides, I got my hands, little brother. I can show them."

Martin appeared totally convinced.

Hennie looked around. "Good thing we got a corn broom, at least. This house sure needs a lot of cleaning, Mom."

Gerda suddenly heard strange voices coming from nearby. Farmer Joe Atkens and his wife, the couple who had sponsored the OpdenDries family for one year to work the forty-acre sugar beet field and help on their two hundred head cattle operation, had come to meet their new employees. They stepped into the kitchen area.

The farmer was a small burly man in his mid-fifties with a sheepish smile. He had a gentle, kind face with clear blue eyes. His head of pitch black hair, with a few swathes of silver running through it, looked like it had been cut with the help of a soup bowl.

Atkens looked at Derk for just a short moment. Suddenly his teeth bared into a widening grin and he slowly held out his hand. It was not a strong handshake. The farmer pushed his hat back, picked a pebble off the floor, and turned it in his fingers as if looking for something to do rather than talk with a man he could not understand.

The farmer took a pipe out of his pocket and lit it with an old lighter. He puffed out a cloud of smoke, his face expressionless. He slowly removed his pipe from his mouth, his white teeth flashing a wide grin.

"How are y'all?" Atkens glanced from one face to the next around the circle. He grunted and made a waving motion in the direction of his farm animals, as if he were immensely gratified at what he had just seen.

His wife was a bird-like woman in her mid-fifties, with dark eyes like a gypsy. She regarded Gerda unsmilingly. Biting her lip, her eyes darted from one to the other. Her gaze eventually settled on Gerda. Mrs. Atkens' mouth tightened, not in an unfriendly manner. There wasn't much of her, but her eyes revealed a core of steel inside. Her clothes were unfashionable and worn. She was not what one would call pretty, with a rough-skinned little face, but she had a sweet expression and a certain kind of sympathy and understanding. When Gerda looked at the woman, she felt as though the tiny woman was on her side.

The farmer's wife shrugged her shoulders suddenly. She put her head to one side, reached her hand towards Gerda, and smiled kindly. "Hello," she said with a little giggle, then brushed past Gerda to stand beside her husband.

Gerda's own smile reached her eyes. The couple's faces had something in common, a kind of beauty. They were both deeply wrinkled and weathered with age, clear-eyed, and filled with peace and kindness.

Is this what farm life does to people in this country? Gerda wondered.

Atkens grabbed hold of Derk's hand once more. Derk felt the rough dry palm rub against his soft hand. He looked straight in the farmer's eyes. Derk noticed the man's leathered face was sagging in both corners.

This man's been working hard, Derk pondered.

Atkens threw a quick look at the boys standing beside Derk. A sly smile crossed his face. He grunted something like, "Good, good! Six come to work for me tomorrow." He looked at Cris to interpret these words.

The farmer tapped Derk on the right shoulder and abruptly broke out in a broad smile. "This is your home. Good home!" He kept his right eye staring in the opposite direction from where the left eye was aiming at. He was somewhat cross-eyed. Derk had a hard time figuring out which direction he was to pay attention.

Atkens got excited. He tipped the huge, chewed-up overhang on his flat, pancake-like dark blue cap and started waving his right arm in a prestigious manner, as if he were showing a luxurious mansion to the OpdenDries family. "Yes, Mr. OpdenDries, this is your home!"

Both his eyes were looking in different directions again, one eye towards the north and the other off in an easterly direction.

Gerda heard some snickering beside her. It was coming from the boys. "You all, get going," she said softly. The boys walked away slowly to start figuring out what household items on the back of the truck should go where and in what house.

The farmer was acting as if these two little ramshackle buildings were expensive mansions, but Gerda, Hennie, and Jodi felt as if they had been dumped in the middle of a no man's land.

Derk tried to think of enough English words to communicate with the farmer, but he couldn't, so they all stood silently waiting for Cris to speak.

"Yep, nice ol' country kitchen," Cris finally said. "Yep! Sure thing, I say. Sure thing."

Gerda took a second look at the bare, grubby walls around her. She got that special kind of look in her eyes again, as if she had something important to say, then decided to strike while the iron was hot. She walked towards the farmer. "You give me paint. We brush, brush!" Gerda made sweeping motions up and down, as if she were painting already. "We good. Very, very good!" She said it with an awkward giggle.

Cris spoke again, but Gerda couldn't figure out what he's said.

The farmer nodded, then said, "Tomorrow?" Atkens tried to look straight ahead, but failed miserably.

"Yes, yes!" Gerda produced her Sunday best smile.

Gerda did a quick reckoning about seating arrangements as Cris brought in four chairs off the truck. She glanced outside, seeing ten apple crates piled under the porch roof. "Those crates will have to do for chairs for a few months until we get our own furniture."

Atkens motioned to Derk, then pointed his index finger towards the stove. "This stove never goes out of this house," he said. "In this country, a warm summer-like day in April can turn into a blizzard the next." He grinned mysteriously. Derk and Gerda did not know what the man was talking about, but Cris made grunting noises indicating his agreement.

The farmer waved his hand for Derk and the boys to come along with him. "Come along. I want to show you the farm."

All the new employees followed the farmer and his wife, who galloped like a racehorse down the narrow pathway. The rest followed like tame sheep.

Gerda saw a trickle of ashes leading towards the back door, indicating someone had tried to clean out those ashes recently. A couple of dusty pictures, curled at the edges, hung on the wall to the left of the cook stove. Directly behind the stove, the farmer had nailed six big spikes in the wall. Two big, dented cooking utensils and four small pans hung on the spikes. Gerda shivered as she stopped to observe a big frying pan hung about two feet above the floor. A big empty syrup tin was placed right under the pan to catch fat drippings. A few thick grease lines showed on the wall. Gerda felt ill. Her stomach churned.

Derk gently nudged her to follow the farmer. Gerda turned. "No, Derk. I'll stay home with Hennie. There's so much to be arranged still."

Derk saw the farmer's house and the farm buildings, which were about a five-minute walk through the farmer's field. He followed his boys down the narrow path through the forty-acre sugar beet field.

Cris was waiting for Derk up a ways. Cris had not said much for a while, but deep down he felt pressed for valuable time. He started making a few noises with his tongue. "I think we better catch up to the farmer. Up there, Derk." Cris waved his crooked finger in the direction the farmer had disappeared in. "We need to find out what's up for work tomorrow. Let's go follow him, quick!"

The newly employed Derk OpdenDries, and six of his sons, and Hennie's boyfriend Henk made a long line following their new farm master, Mr. Joe Atkens.

The farmer led them to a barn where he kept two hundred cattle. Directly across from the cattle barn, he had three farrowing barns with one hundred fifty sows and another two large holding barns for feeder pigs.

Once Cris had explained to Derk the farmer's wishes for the following day, Atkens began giving salutes with the two fingers on his right hand, as if he'd been a soldier at one time. "See you at six in the morning." He smiled, turned, and walked towards his home, which looked like an ancient, fallen down castle. Cris, Derk, and the boys all walked back home.

Meanwhile, Gerda and Hennie checked out the second home, which was not much better than the first. Inside, they saw four double beds stacked up on top of each other like bunk beds. The rooms had two small linen closets. There was no heat.

"We will use this house to sleep all the boys," Gerda decided quickly.

She walked outside. Once again, she clasped her hands in front of her. With her head inclined to one side, she pondered the basic needs of her family to survive the next two months. How could she organize these lone, dirty old houses with the goods they had available to them? A sudden twitch of her right cheek betrayed her inner struggle. Gerda felt tears resurface. Agitated at her own weakness, Gerda quick wiped away a few tears trickling down her cheeks.

Derk came home and stood beside her. He put his arm around her shoulders as they each sorted out their own frustrations. Again, Derk gazed in disbelief at the jumbled, uneven roofs and the two doors hanging crazily on their hinges. Derk thought of Holland, where work, people, and managing a big organization had been his everyday business. This was so very different.

Has it been the right move for my family, for Gerda?

Derk wondered in silence just how things for him and their family would look like some twenty years from now. A sigh escaped his tight-pressed lips.

Both Derk and Gerda stood like two lost souls trying to put everything into realistic perspective. In this new country, there was so much to learn.

Derk squeezed Gerda's hand. "I guess I've got to pay my dues to learn about farming in this new country." He let out a soft snicker, but it was not from happiness. "I've got to get me a radio to learn the English language soon, Gerda. Real soon, I say."

Henk, holding Hennie's hand, and the older boys saw the struggle taking place in the hearts of the two silent figures in front of the weather-beaten houses they'd all be living in. One by one, they came to stand beside Derk and Gerda.

Gerda could not help but share how homesick she was for Holland and the feeling of security they'd left behind to try to find a better future. A sudden serene silence blanketed the group.

Derk looked at the children standing around them. He took a deep breath, then cleared his throat softly. "A long time ago, my own father told me, 'Derk, you will not be judged in life by how you handle your successes, but how you deal with your disappointments.'" Derk looked sideways. He let his eyes rest on Gerda. "I guess that could help us in this situation, too. You think so, Gerda?"

Derk left no time for her to answer him. He suddenly threw his fine head up high, and gently lifted Gerda's chin to look deep into her eyes. He squeezed both her hands. "Don't you worry, Gerda. We're in this together. All of us."

Gerda blinked back a few nasty teardrops. Her eyes were strained. There was shock and hurt in her face at the unexpected upheaval they were now faced with. She withdrew from Derk's grip and slowly looked around the circle of her loved ones. Gerda tensely assessed the difficult situation confronting them.

Suddenly, her heartbeat returned to normal. Gerda managed a warm smile and, with a firm nod of the head that sent the last few tears scrambling down her pale cheeks, she looked deep into Derk's eyes, where she recognized her husband's genuine concern for her happiness. Her deep blue eyes, which earlier had shown deep despair, now shone with a fighting spirit that lay deep within her soul.

Memories stirred the back of her consciousness and she felt tears prickling the back of her eyes again. *What will I hold onto? Good memories from the past? Or will I choose to try to make a cozy home and atmosphere for all of us here?*

Derk watched as the corners of her mouth began to twitch.

Gerda suddenly shifted her right foot, and with a quick swipe of the back of her right hand she wiped the last few tears from her eyes. *I can do two things: either crumple under the strain and pressure, pouting over the loss of former comforts, or show the core of steel inside me and become an example of reassurance to the whole family.*

Gerda slowly raised her head up high. With a firm set of the jaw, she looked around the circle, then upwards to Derk. "I think we've come a long, long way to experience this new adventure, Derk." She paused. "We're not giving up this easy, are we?" She spoke with controlled emotions. Her eyes illuminated a jolly twinkle, for the first time in a long while.

Derk saw the sparkle in the previously tortured eyes of his wife. He threw his head back. The corners of his mouth twitched upward before he let his deep, roaring laughter roll over the lone prairie—a healthy laughter that indicated triumph over the fear, regret, and doubt which had nearly taken his joy in life away.

He turned to face his wife. "Gerda, do you suppose we relegated God into being our co-pilot? If so, perhaps we should switch seats with Him right this very moment." He held out his hand towards her, then lifted her chin and looked deep into her eyes. "We are not going to bend like a willow before the winds of misfortune." He looked to look around the circle of children standing around them. "Are we now?"

Gerda took hold of his hand. Her darting eyes expressed deep understanding. "Life is not so much about waiting for the storm to pass as it is about learning how to dance in the storm," she said softly. "But it is mighty hard to dance at this time, Derk. Awful hard, indeed."

All she could muster was a tapping of her right foot on the hard clay soil.

After that first evening, when the wobbling sun melted into wide pools of brilliant orange-red and the wind dropped to a steady moan, the two lone houses in southern Alberta would never to be the same again. The sedate town of Picture Butte, where life had been slow, orderly and unruffled, would see a noticeable change once the OpdenDries brothers started using the long, dusty roads and wide open spaces to master their Ford cars, Chevy trucks, four-wheeled tractors, and wild horses.

Later that evening, when the winds whispered around the eaves of their new dwelling place, Gerda lay awake thinking of Holland and the son they had left behind.

14

True Grit!

The day dawned clear and cool. The sun was in hiding still, itching to spread its warming rays across the whole wide world. It was a perfect day in nature.

Gerda was not the type of woman to shy away from a new adventure.

The OpdenDries family had now lived in the tiny houses for two weeks. Things were improving. Gerda, Hennie, and Jodi had been scrubbing and cleaning everyday from morning till evening, stripping wallpaper, whitewashing walls and ceilings, cleaning windows, painting woodwork, and scrubbing the floors in every room.

Derk and Hennie had gone with the farmer's tractor and a wagon to a machinery auction sale where they bought a dresser with four drawers, two pairs of curtains, a metal barrel to store drinking water, and some groceries for the week to come.

Just three days before, a horrendous rainfall had come along. Gerda, Hennie, and Jodi gathered every pot and pan they could find to catch drips of water coming through the ceilings in both houses.

Farmer Atkens said he would get a carpenter to fix the roof and the cracks around the windows.

Two days before, Gerda and Hennie had spent all day washing the laundry. There was no clean water anywhere nearby. Derk and the boys got ten pails full of water out of a huge irrigation ditch running close by their place. They poured all the water into a big wooden tub that Mina, Derk's sister, had given Gerda to use for washing.

Gerda boiled ditch water each morning. The boys would bring three pails full of water to the house before they left for work. She stored the boiling water in the new water barrel that Derk had bought at the auction sale.

Mina had shown Gerda that the dirt had to be paddled out of the work clothes and then boiled in soapy water in big iron pots. Gerda and Hennie took turns stirring the clothes with a big stick. Then they had to be rinsed and hung out to dry on a clothesline that Derk had strung up between the two houses.

Gerda used the same irrigation reservoir water for drinking and cooking their food. The murky ditch water had to be filtered and cooked for twenty minutes before anyone could drink it.

The day before, Hennie and Jodi had spent all day heating irons on the stove and ironing dresses, white shirts to wear to church on Sunday, bed linens, and aprons.

This morning, at six o'clock in the morning, Gerda stood by the porch door to watch Derk and his sons walk down a narrow path through the field until they disappeared behind the cattle shed on Joe Atkens' farmyard.

Gerda spent a little extra time enjoying the first sunrays as they paint their soft golden beauty above the far horizon. A soft smile crossed her face as a new plan sprung to life within her. Derk and the five oldest boys had been working on the farm feeding cattle and pigs, cleaning barns, and oiling greasing farm implements. Those implements were to be used for ploughing the fields, seeding oats and barley, and planting forty acres of sugar beets in a few weeks.

Gerda walked inside the house and poured herself another cup of leftover coffee. She sat down on a wooden chair by the kitchen table and stared at the bare walls and the eight apple crates they used for chairs. *It's a far cry from the cozy neat kitchen I left behind,* she thought with a sigh.

Gerda sank her chin into her chest, but only for a moment. Sound reasoning soon took over, as if she had found within herself undreamed-of resources of courage and resolution. *There are only two ways I can tackle this problem. One is to feel sorry for myself, heaven forbid, and the other is to try making the best of what we have to work with.*

She squared her shoulder and stood up straight, finishing her coffee. *Get thee behind me, Satan! You may not yet understand, but I, Gerda, refuse to be shackled down by the good things we left behind.* A mischievous look enlivened her fatigued face. *Let's go see how I can drive away these blues today.* The courageous mother of ten, who had lived through five war-torn years, revived her natural sense of humour once again.

At first, everything in this country had been so different that it confused her. But now, a few weeks later, life in the two lone prairie houses had settled into a fairly regular routine.

Gerda walked towards the porch and looked out the window towards Joe Atkens' farm buildings, where Derk and the boys were busy working. Gerda smiled as she recollected Mina's last visit with them.

"You must sew cotton underwear for the boys, Gerda," she'd said. "Those heavy Dutch ones are way too warm in the summertime out here in Canada." Mina had waved her crooked little finger under her nose. "And Gerda! This old sewing machine of mine? It is a Singer! The best there is in the world!"

Mina had marched to the family car and come back with a stack of linen. "Tell you what," she'd said. "Here's twenty Robin Hood flour sacks for you to sew the boys summer underwear. Been saving them for two years already." Mina cautiously let her fingers run across a Robin Hood face printed on the top piece of material. "Here, Gerda, for you. Ready to use!" Mina nodded her head. She spoke in soft, glum tones as if it was hard for her to part with her treasure.

"Gerda, it's… it's strong, durable cotton." The wrinkles in her face deepened. She'd taken a deep breath. "You'll be able to sew at least eight sets of shorts out of this pile of material, you hear? It's… it's a whole twenty flour sacks I have given you, Gerda. Twenty, I say!" Mina stood by the material as if she were going to a funeral.

Gerda abruptly turned and sat down by the table again. She saw soft sunbeams come through the window pane and shine onto the big yellow and white bouquet of wild prairie flowers Jodi had put on the windowsill before helping Hennie make the beds in the "sleep room" next door.

She slowly looked around the dark, dreary kitchen as though she was seeing it for the first time. She got up from her chair with that familiar spirit of grit and courage. *I'll go and see what we can do to this dark hole.*

With her chin thrust forward, she hustled to the bedroom and knocked on the bedroom door. "Hennie, Jodi, wake up! We need to go shopping right early today."

Gerda made a grocery list and discussed some of the things they needed to buy while Hennie and Jodi ate their breakfast. She put the list in the pocket of her dress.

She glanced up at the clock. It was eight o'clock already. "We best hurry along so we can do some sewing later today."

"But Mom, we don't even know how to talk English," Jodi snickered softly.

Gerda looked out the kitchen window down the three-mile road that arched its way around a big lake close to the town of Picture Butte. She could see the town in the distance.

Her face lit up with a broad grin. "Guess we will need to let our fingers do the talking, like this!" Gerda pretended that she was sorting groceries and counting spools of thread. Then she sat down on a kitchen chair and imitated the peddling of a sewing machine.

Hennie and Jodi let out a peel of delightful laughter.

Gerda clasped her hands in front of her, the motion she always made when she was inspired to undertake a worthy assignment. "Go, get the bikes, you two. Hurry! We'll need to bike three miles round the lake to get to town." She looked up at the clock. "That should take us a good forty minutes."

"Fine. Jodi can sit on the back of my bike, Mom," Hennie chuckled.

Gerda was glad her brother-in-law, Cris, had given them two bicycles. Distances in this country were spread far too wide apart to get much done by walking.

Once Gerda and the girls were halfway down the road, the sun started beating down on them. It was going to be a warm day. She'd heard so much about grocery shopping in Canada. Even though she would not have very much money to spend, never mind for anything fancy, it would feel great just to browse around.

This trip, to Gerda, meant much more than exploring, though. It was their very first shopping adventure in a new homeland. Yes, she was going to teach her two girls how to get along with people in a land where none of them had any idea how to communicate with the clerk behind the counter.

Gerda stopped to wipe her brow. A southern breeze began rippling the placid lake water between sparsely grown bushes near the edge. Hennie and Jodi were way up ahead already. She quickly jumped on her bike again, biting her lip as she peddled hard to catch up.

Near town, a horse and buggy passed by. The man and wife in the buggy smiled and waved.

Once they were out of sight, Gerda heard a loud noise. A freight truck was coming towards them up the road from town. The truck window was caked full of mud, and there was only a small peek hole wiped clean from dirt through which the driver could see the road in front of him. Gerda watched, horrified. The truck swerved sideways and nearly forced Hennie and Jodi off the side of the road.

Gerda slipped off her own bike and pulled it into the ditch with her. The truck whizzed by, its tires whipping a thick layer of dust in her direction. Fine sand hit the side of her face, tightening her throat. Gerda could not see momentarily.

"Wait up, Hennie," she tried to scream, but her voice choked. She started coughing, shaking with fear and exhaustion.

Hennie and Jodi waited for her a little ways down the road. Gerda immediately grabbed hold of her emotions. She stared down the road and saw the two chimneys of the sugar beet factory to the left of them.

Huge white letters spelling "Picture Butte" were painted on a tall, deep red wheat granary nearby.

Gerda sighed. Hennie and Jodi had not seen her near collision with the truck. Gerda was not about to let her girls see her anger. She smiled instead. "Let's take a breather. It's been a long time since I biked, you know?"

The three sat on the side of the road. "I wonder what school will be like," said thirteen-year-old Jodi.

"I guess you will find out soon," Hennie said. "It must be fun learning a new language and all."

Gerda's eyes twinkled with anticipation. "Best we get going. Let's go find out what shopping is like in town."

A few minutes later, the trio biked through the dusty, snaggle-toothed, one-horse buggy town. None of the buildings seemed to be looked after. They hobbled across a railroad track and reached the centre of Picture Butte.

The three new visitors stopped to survey their surroundings. There was a barber shop, a grocery store, and a post office on one side of the street. The other side had a noisy saloon, a feed mill, and an automotive garage with three Model-A cars and a couple of Chevy pick-up trucks scattered at the end of the street.

Gerda noticed a dozen low-roofed wooden homes built around the town with no particular rhyme or reason to any of it. Right at the end of what she supposed could be the main street, there was a government house and a neatly white-painted Presbyterian church. There was a small bookstore wedged between a saddle store and grocery store.

Gerda saw a flat-roofed building with a long row of small windows on the south side, facing the centre of town.

"That must be the Picture Butte schoolhouse," she said to Hennie.

There was not much colour to this prairie settlement. The shabbily built dwellings reminded her of a community where nobody was yet fully committed to staying for good. They seemed to want to be able to move on without leaving too much behind.

"Come, let's go now." Gerda went ahead, walking her bike across a wooden sidewalk with tufts of wild grasses sticking through worn-out planks here and there. *Grass must grow plentiful in here.*

She headed for what looked to be the grocery store. Gerda smiled and placed her bicycle by the wall, then hopped over a few broken wooden planks in the sidewalk until she reached the front door. Gerda turned the door-knob. The door opened only halfway. She gave the door another push. The hinges creaked as if they were crying for a squirt of oil. The trio sauntered through the long, low-roofed store.

Gerda come to sudden halt in the middle of the small store. She looked around, as if she were expecting that all her grocery items would be displayed on nice, clean, painted shelving. There was none of that. Instead there was a jumbled arrangement of groceries, hardware, linens, dishes, and pots and pans scattered about on long dusty planks along the wall behind a rough wooden counter.

Gerda come to a complete standstill. She quickly glanced over the jumbled arrangement, then closed her eyes, looking as if she were praying. Her face reddened from the base of her neck upwards.

Jodi saw her mother close her eyes and wanted to snicker, but she did not dare. *Mom's not happy. I better stay quiet.*

Hennie also watched her mom's unusual reaction. She walked up to Gerda and gave her a big hug. "Don't worry, Mom. We'll find the things we need, I am sure." On second thought, she was not so sure herself.

Gerda did not reply immediately. Only the strain in her eyes and her faint smile betrayed the inner struggle raging inside. Gerda pressed her lips into a perfect circle that usually indicated she was calculating how to tackle a difficult situation. When she finally spoke, it was in a soft tone. "This is not what I had expected, girls. Never, ever!"

In her frustration, Gerda did not notice a woman in her fifties parading behind the long, narrow counter, chewing gum and opening a chocolate bar at the same time. The tall, high-bosomed woman, with a healthy set of round, cherry-coloured cheeks, looked like a model of prosperity in size and well-rounded measurements. She towered above Gerda, looking down at her new customer as she engulfed a few inches of the chocolate bar in her hands. The lady marched back and forth behind the counter as if she were very busy with the business of running a country grocery store. A huge mass of long, dark brown curls fell around her face in ringlets. They bounced up and down each time her heavy footsteps hit the floor.

The clerk paused momentarily to observe Gerda and the girls from behind gold-rimmed spectacles that rested comfortably on the bridge of her nose. It was not that she was terribly ugly, but the large underchin that hit her bosom at regular intervals as she paraded behind the counter was a most unusual sight.

Gerda could not help but smirk when the woman's voice came whistling through a set of pure white teeth surrounded by brightly coloured red lips. "How can I serve you, madam?" she asked in English.

"Me no understand," Gerda managed.

The clerk cupped an ear with her hands and looked at Gerda. The repeated incredulous glances that were exchanged back and forth between them made Gerda realize that this woman was trying her level best to be helpful to them. There was a long pause as the clerk looked at Gerda as though she were something new and incredible she'd never seen before. Then she directed her large hand in Gerda's direction and proceeded with a forceful handshake. Hennie and Jodi watched Gerda's eyes close under the pressure.

"Oh, you must be the new immigrants at Mr. Atkens' farm over there." The clerk pointed in the direction they had come from.

Gerda was unprepared for the power of the grip, so when the clerk kept pumping her hand, a look of despair replaced her friendly smile. The stout woman seemed certain that she had been successful in her attempt to be friendly to this new immigrant family that had come to Picture Butte from a faraway land.

Just when Gerda was about to buckle under the pressure to her hand, the clerk released her powerful grip. Gerda started rubbing her hand to stimulate the blood circulation.

Oh, if I could only talk to her, Gerda thought.

She took a few steps back, seeing flour, sugar, and beans in one corner of the store. In yet another corner, she saw knitting and sewing materials and paper products stacked away on a shelf above twenty-five-pound bags of Robin Hood flour. Those bags had paintings of a little green man on the front, just like the ones Mina had given her last week.

Gerda walked over to that corner. She ran her fingers through the sewing materials, picking out white, red, and black sewing thread. She placed all of this on the counter and raised her index finger to the middle of her chest. She nodded her head. "Me taken this."

Calm came over Gerda. She did not feel rushed any longer, having learned many years ago that wise decisions, and sensible purchases, had to be done with the greatest care. She extracted her grocery list from her dress pocket and started looking around calmly. Gerda opened her mouth to speak, then appeared to change her mind and turned around.

When she could not find what she was looking for, she tapped the clerk on her right shoulder.

Gerda's creative mind shifted into high gear. She hunched down on her heels. "See, see?" Gerda clenched her hand into a solid fist and started making squeezing motions as if she were milking a cow.

"Yes," the clerk said with a smile. "Milk from the cow!"

"Ja... ja!" Gerda was pleased with her achievement, but she was not nearly finished yet. She walked to the back of the store and picked up a corn broom. She tipped the broom upside-down and started turning the handle round and round as if she were stirring.

The girls watched Gerda's face turn beet-red from the hard work before she let go with one hand and pretended to dip down with the other. Gerda raised the dipped finger to her mouth. She said, "Jum... Jum!"

The clerk chuckled loudly. "Yes, yes. Butter! We have!"

Gerda got braver still. She tapped the clerk's shoulder one more time. She cupped her hands around her mouth and blew out her cheeks until they looked like two little red apples. She blew puffs of air towards the clerk across the counter.

Poised intently, the clerk shifted from one foot to the other, anticipating another clue to the puzzle.

Gerda started patting one hand on top of the other half a dozen times before changing to a kneading motion that was followed by a rolling gesture as if she were producing nice round balls for baking bread. Gerda turned and pretended to be opening a hot oven door. She lifted her eyes towards the clerk. "Warm... warm."

The clerk nodded vigorously. "Yes… yes, bread! We have!"

Gerda showed ten fingers on her hands. "This much, please."

"Yes… yes." The clerk disappeared behind a creaky door. She came back with ten loaves of bread. She made another trip to the back and promptly produced four bottles of milk and two pounds of butter.

"Good, good," Gerda chuckled. "We come back to you."

The clerk made out a bill. Gerda checked the bill and smiled. "Yes, good. I pay now."

Gerda looked to Hennie and Jodi. "At least the numbers look the same as in Holland," Gerda chuckled.

Hennie and Jodi were already busy packing the groceries into the two big Robin Hood flour bags they had brought along. Gerda paid the clerk seven dollars, turned, and walked to the door. She turned around by the door once more before leaving.

"Adieu!" she said, hoping the clerk could understand a bit of French.

Once they got home, Gerda felt dog tired from the shopping adventure. After a cup of warm tea, she asked Hennie to help put Mina's Singer sewing machine near the window. "You and Jodi help me make shorts for the boys."

Hennie and Jodi made sure that the Robin Hood faces stayed in one piece while Hennie started cutting the materi al. "Make sure you don't cut away the Robin Hood noses, Jodi," Hennie mused.

When Derk and the boys came home at suppertime, Derk saw Gerda behind the sewing machine on a table by the bedroom window. Beads of perspiration dripped off the tip of her nose.

Derk washed his hands, then walked over to his wife. "You should not be working so hard, Gerda. You know things go wrong when trying too hard."

She looked up. "I shouldn't? Your sister Mina has been telling me the suffering heat you and the boys will be going through when those sugar beets need cleaning and thinning out this summer."

Gerda ever so gently stroked the Robin Hood face on the first finished pair of sewn underwear. She looked up at Derk. "Mina says white cotton is supposed to be a lot cooler on hot summer days than the heavy underwear we have brought along from Holland." Gerda's eyes twinkled with sheer delight.

When Derk and the boys came home from work the next day, they saw a long line of brand new washed underwear hanging on the clothesline outside. Smiling Robin Hood faces, some with the feathers on their green hats chopped down a bit, were swinging back and forth in the soft, muttering wind.

Some of the boys made fun of the little green men. Gerda paid no attention to such gobbledygook. She turned around swiftly. "Tomorrow I must teach my girls how to bake bread in a wood stove oven." She was speaking more to herself than to anyone else.

Gerda felt proud of her newfound skills on how to make cookies, cake, and bread in a wood stove, something she'd never done before.

15

Snowstorm

It was warm, sunny, and bright when Bert and Jodi biked to school. The sun was hanging peacefully in a sky filled with little clouds jostling for positioning. The wind was calm and the roads clear. There was not a trace of bad weather coming their way.

"Mom, can Jodi and I bike to school this morning?" Bert asked at the breakfast table.

Gerda nodded. "Can't see why not. It's not too cold or windy. Sure, go ahead. But be sure to take care of Jodi, remember?"

Little did the new immigrants know that a pleasant, warm early spring day on the wide open prairie could change into a howling blizzard in the blink of an eye.

Uncle Cris had warned Derk some time ago to put a large coil of binder twine on a big spike between the two houses, just in case a blizzard popped up in a raging hurry.

"You just take the roll of twine, uncoiling it as you go, to the other house or to the farm in the morning, so that if you miss the barn or the house you just pull yourselves back holding the strong string to get back," Cris had said. "Then you go try once more. You won't get lost then. Believe me, Derk, people die every year when one of those nasty blizzards comes along."

When Bert and Jodi biked into town, they passed a row of silent houses that looked peaceful and quiet under a thick layer of snow over the huddled roofs. Here and there, thick clusters of smoke came out of the chimneys and went straight up into the mild, frosty sky.

Bert and Jodi stepped off their bikes and hurried around the back of the school. Suddenly, a strong northeasterly wind caught them off-guard, as though someone had thrown a bucket of ice cubes on top their heads.

Bert, who had been exposed to the cold winds before while working with the boys on the farm, sensed it would be tough to get home. He looked up and saw ragged clouds begin to scurry about in wild, swirling motions in the same sky that had been so peaceful and quiet a few moments ago.

It looks like snow is coming our way. Maybe the teacher will let us go home early, Bert hoped.

Bert noticed a strong northeast wind blowing. Soon he paid little attention to what the teacher was saying.

Snowflakes were forcing their way through the narrow crack under the door close to where he sat. Bert looked around, seeing fancy frost flowers starting to cover the five small windows facing the north side of the school. He squinted his eyes, trying to see through the only clear spot left in the middle of the window. Through it, he saw loose snow whirling up against the doors and windows of a half-dozen wooden shacks across the street.

The warm breeze from the south must have changed direction to the north! It will be hard to bike around the lake in this wind.

Bert heard the wind unleash another howling gust. A worried look framed his young face. How could it be? This morning, it had taken him and his sister only half an hour to bike around the Picture Butte lake. Now, he didn't know *how* he was going to get home.

Bert shifted around in his school desk, then glanced over to Jodi two benches over. Again he heard the fierce wind whistling loudly outside. Oh, how he wished his teacher would let them go home early. Bert bit his tongue, resting his face in the palm of his hands.

The school teacher heard a strong wind shake the wood frame building. He got off his chair and walked to the nearest window, where he scraped a small hole in the frost to peer outside. Next, he walked to the door and turned the knob. He heaved his strong body against it, but it only opened halfway. An icy wind slapped him in the face. A sudden cold draft filled the small room as he quickly closed the door.

"Blizzard!" he muttered under his breath.

Back at his desk, he looked over the heads of his twenty-five students. A worried look came over his face.

How will these youngsters get home safely? he wondered. To make matters even worse, he had seen a dozen of them come biking to school that morning.

He rapped his knuckles on the desk. "Listen! It looks like the beginnings of a bad snowstorm. I want everyone to hurry on home, quick! Put your coats on and dress warm, you hear?" He tried to disguise his worry. "Go straight home, hurry! Before the storm gets worse."

Deep down inside, he knew this type of storm had been the cause of death more than once. Why, even the previous year a father and son had been found frozen along the main road close by the Picture Butte lake.

Bert jumped to his feet instantly and grabbed his coat and toque off the hook on the wall. He walked towards Jodi. "Wait here by the steps for me, Jodi. I'll go get your bike!"

Bert rushed out the door, pulling his toque deep over his ears. Bert was the first by the bicycle shed and had no trouble wheeling Jodi's bike out the door. He breathed in the cold air, then waited impatiently for Jodi to come out the door.

As soon as he saw her come, he shouted, "Best be getting home. Hurry! Mom will be worried about us." He gave Jodi her bike. "Get going! Don't worry about me. I'll catch up to you, ya hear?" There was desperation in his voice.

Jodi, dressed in a red-grey snowsuit with a bright red woollen hat, had warm scarves wrapped around her neck. She slipped her mitts on her hands, gave her bike a shove forward, and jumped on the seat.

"Be careful, Jodi. It's terribly cold out!" Bert hoped she could hear his voice above the howling wind

Bert worked his way towards the shed again. Two bigger boys shoved him aside, grabbing hold of their bikes before Bert could get his own.

Bert finally shoved his bike out the door, quickly pedalling in the direction Jodi had gone down the road. As he got closer, he saw Jodi round the corner onto the main road heading for home.

He tried hard to catch up. A sudden icy gust of wind swept loose snow off the flat-roofed schoolhouse and into his face. He tried peddling faster to catch up to his sister. All he could see was whirling snow clouds whipping across the road in front of him. For a slight moment, he saw Jodi's bright red hat shine through the white snow, but then his sister disappeared in another whiteout.

Jodi, up ahead, had trouble making much headway. The driving winds that came from the northeast blew over the frozen lake kept teasing her cheeks in places her scarves did not cover, and almost tore the handle from her fingers. She stopped to step off her bicycle, then took off her mitts and tried to wrap her scarves more securely around her neck. Her cheeks and fingers started tingling from the cold. She quickly put her mittens back on and got back on the bike.

Meanwhile, Bert caught up to her. His starry blue eyes filled with tears. He tried to coach Jodi to ride in the bike tracks he made ahead of her. "Come on, Jodi. Hurry!" Bert started riding directly in front of her in an effort to break the wind so she could follow him easier.

Jodi bit her lips. A mass of curly blond hair was dancing around her face. She tried hard to bike in the tracks, but after a while she stopped and stepped off her bike again. She was wearing a heavy winter jacket with woollen toque and gloves, but the repeated gusts of wind whipped right down to the bones. The drifting snow had already created a few humps of snow in the middle of the road. It was getting harder to keep up with her brother.

She jumped on her bike to try again, setting her jaw in an effort not to let her tears run down her cheeks and freeze on her cold, blue-coloured cheekbones. The wind struck her in the face. It was an arctic blast screaming from the east, picking up bite as it drove over the frozen lake. She'd never give up, though—never!

Only half-seeing between the weaving veils of blustery snow that came drifting off the lake in wild and furious flurries across the road, Bert and Jodi struggled to keep their balance. A little more than halfway around the lake, it became increasingly hard to peddle their bikes. Bert felt the cold sear through his clothing. He was so afraid the blinding snow would make his sister run her bike off the road and into the ditch. Bert turned around on his bike as best he could.

"Try to stay close to me, Jodi!"

Bert tried to see if his wheels were still making wide enough tracks for Jodi to follow him, but no sooner had he made a narrow trail than the northeast wind wiped away all trace of it.

Bert rounded the last curve close to home. The snow had become a thick, blinding storm. He felt his feet freezing, cold as ice. There was a funny numbness creeping up both his legs. The sharp shooting pains he'd felt earlier in both ears were gone now. Bert looked back to locate his sister.

Jodi had fallen behind steadily. Bert could barely see her anymore. Fear gripped his soul. *Mom told me to look after Jodi. I've got to get home to get help for her! She'll never make it!*

Bert felt warm tears stinging the back of his eyes. His face was purple-blue from the cold, but he knew crying was not going to help. *I have to get home to get help, now! For Jodi's sake!*

Bert saw his home dimly emerging ahead of him in the swirling white haze. With a new burst of hope and energy, his frozen feet managed to keep pumping the bike pedals. He pushed even harder, feeling every intake of breath sting as if a thistle was piercing his lungs over and over again. His cry pierced the frozen surroundings—"Help, help!" But no one heard his cry.

Gerda, at home, paced the floor. She didn't know much about Canadian winters, but this had to be an unusual kind of winter storm. Surely, somebody would be bringing the children who biked to school to their homes by bus or car, wouldn't they? It would only be common sense!

The weather had changed so suddenly. Gerda stopped by the window to clear a small patch on the frozen window pane. She tried seeing through the whirling snow in hopes of catching sight of her two youngest come down the road. Gerda blew again and again against the window so that she could have a better view outside.

She glanced up at the clock. It was only two o'clock. Bert and Jodi never came home from school this early, but with weather like this? *Why wasn't there a warning of some sort? How can the weather change so quickly? Is this normal in Canada?*

Gerda sank to her knees to pray. Hennie, sensing her crisis, knelt beside her and put her arm around her mother's shoulders. "Lord, please let these little ones come home safely… all of our family… I beg of You!" Tears started flowing down both her cheeks.

Suddenly she heard a loud stamping of feet outside. Gerda and Hennie heard loud voices.

"Dad and the boys must be home, Hennie! Quick! Open the door!"

A strong gust of wind accompanied Derk and the boys coming through the door.

"Are Bert and Jodi home yet?" Derk's voice sounded anxious with fear. He looked at the snow blowing in through gaping cracks around the windows and the door. The snow had settled in a long white line by the door.

Gerda's voice choked. "No, Derk. I can't even see them coming down the road!"

Derk swallowed hard. "The weather turned awful bad real quick, Gerda." He began pacing the floor. "If the teacher sent them home early, they must be out there on the road somewhere!" He tossed his head in Gerda's and the boys' direction. There was a resolute expression in his eyes. "Tom, Martin, come with me at once. We must find them. Quick!"

Both the boys, still dressed in winter clothing, hurried outside. By the door, Derk looked at his younger sons. "Marcel, Dick, take care of business down here!" Derk pulled his woollen hat over his ears. "Stoke up the fire, you hear?"

Tom and Martin stood waiting for Derk outside the door. "Hurry. Let's go, Dad. Bert and Jodi could freeze to death!" Martin grabbed hold of Derk's shoulder. "Come! Now!"

The three hooked their arms together. With bent heads, they started walking against the northeast wind, feeling the icy gusts driving them from the back.

Derk lifted his head, coming out of the driveway. He looked down the road. Suddenly he saw Bert come coming towards them out of a white, swirling haze of snow.

"There's Bert!" he yelled. "Hurry!"

But Martin and Tom had already forced their way forward to go help their little brother.

When Bert saw his dad and brothers, a sudden lame feeling came over him. He felt dizzy and collapsed. Derk caught his youngest son into his arms.

Feeling his dad's strong arms around him, Bert lifted his weary eyes. "Jodi, Dad, she's still out there." Bert tried lifting his right arm to point down the road. He could not move his arms. "She… she couldn't make it, Dad." Warm tears trickled down his frozen face. It felt as if every muscle in his body were frozen solid. "I couldn't wait for her, Dad. I had to go get help. Someone has to go get her, Dad. Hurry."

Derk felt Bert's body shivering in his arms.

Martin and Tom were already hurrying down the road.

"Go on, Dad, take Bert home! We'll go get Jodi!" Tom shouted, already following Martin down the road.

Derk turned his back against the wind. "How far, Bert? How far down the road is she?"

"Round the bend, Dad, last time I saw her…" Bert cast tear-filled eyes upwards one more time. His body started shivering wildly. "Will they find her, Dad? Will they?" Bert let his pent-up tears stream down his frozen cheeks.

Derk tried pulling Bert's bike off the road. "Yes, Bert. You know Tom and Martin are strong! I know they'll bring Jodi home." Derk spoke loudly, hoping his half-frozen son would hear.

"Oh, good," Bert sighed. He felt his dad's strong arms around him. Then there was darkness all around.

Jodi, meanwhile, used every ounce of energy in her body to try keeping up with Bert. She struggled her way around the last bend in the road, feeling numb and frozen. She bit her lip. Her feet would not move anymore. She could not coordinate her thoughts. She started to cry. Through her tear-filled eyes, she saw snowdrifts piled up across the road. The fierce wind and swirling snow were choking her.

Jodi tried to screw the knuckles of her left hand into her eyes to wipe away the tears.

Her body began shivering uncontrollably. Her frozen fingers let go of the handlebar and she fell to the frozen ground with a loud bang. Then there was complete darkness all around. A big blue spot started forming on the side of her head

Her body lay still beside her bike. All was dark. Swirling snowflakes merrily drifted around her pale face.

Jodi's eyelids fluttered open for just a brief moment. She saw two figures hovering over her. She could hardly breathe anymore. "So… so… awful… awful… cold!" she whispered softly.

Tom lifted Jodi off the road. He felt her body trembling in his strong arms. A chill crept through him. "Jodi, my little darling!" He looked at her pure white face and shuddered with unknown fear, frightened that she might not wake up again. Tom hugged her tightly, hoping his body's warmth would help stop her body from shivering. Tom whispered in her right ear, "Jodi, Martin and I are taking you home, home to Mom and Dad!"

"Follow in my footprints, Tom!" Martin shouted to his brother.

From out the bedroom window, Gerda saw Derk coming down the driveway with Bert in his arms. She slipped on her winter coat and ran towards them to help. Hennie held open the door.

Once inside, Derk laid his near-frozen son close by the warm stove. "Best get him warmed up real quick, Gerda. He's a mighty cold boy."

Derk gently removed Bert's toque from his head. He saw two big white spots on both his ears. Suddenly, he was struck with panic.

"Move him away from the hot stove, quick!" he shouted.

Derk ran outside. His brother-in-law, Cris, had told him that any fast thawing on a human body could cause that particular part to fall off completely. He would not let that happen!

Derk scooped two hands full of fresh snow and came back inside the house.

Meanwhile, Johan got a couple of towels and put them around Bert's neck. "Hold still, Bert."

Derk held his cupped, snow-filled hands on Bert's ears until the snow was melted. "Uncle Cris told me that melting snow on frozen parts is the only way to bring back blood circulation to the frozen part of the human body without there being any permanent damage to the skin."

Gerda kept her winter coat on. She paced up and down, from holding Bert's hand to looking out the bedroom window, hoping to see Tom and Martin bring Jodi home.

A sudden shout came from out of the bedroom.

"Derk, they found Jodi!" Gerda raced to the door. "Thank You, Lord, thank You!" she shouted, racing out the door and flying down the road to meet the two boys.

"Go! Help them, Johan!" Derk said. He shoved a warm coat in Johan's arms to go meet his brothers and put the coat over their little sister.

A few moments later, Tom came into the house holding his little sister close to him. He cautiously placed his unconscious sister on his parents' bed. Gerda and Hennie immediately found more warm clothing and began gently rubbing her arms and legs to bring back the blood circulation.

After fifteen minutes, Jodi tried opening her eyelids again, ever so slowly. She tried to move her swollen lips. "Home… Mom?" Her tired eyelids fell shut again.

Once Bert felt tingling come back to his ears again, he threw back the wet towels and jumped to his feet. He looked at Derk and put both his arms around Derk's neck. "Thank you, Dad! Thank you for coming to get me!"

Derk swallowed hard. "You're my son, Bert. My son!" His voice cracked. He put his hand on Bert's shoulder.

Bert tiptoed towards the bed where Jodi lay pale and motionless. She was breathing heavily. Bert touched her right arm gently, his eyes filled with tenderness. "Jodi, we're home! Home… safe with Mom and Dad, Jodi. Safe!" He got up closer to her face and gently kissed her. He whispered in her ear. "I love you, Jodi. Wake up now, please?"

Jodi opened her eyes slowly. She tried recollect what had happened to her. She saw Bert, and then remembered. A sweet smile crossed her face. "Thank you… Bert… Thanks!" Her voice trailed off as she fell asleep again, holding Bert's hand.

Even though the cold winds continued to pick up speed outside, there was a certain closeness amongst the OpdenDries family like never before.

Derk, overlooking his family, broke the silence. "Let's give our heavenly Father all the praise for keeping each one of us safe, secure, and alive." When Derk folded his rough work hands to pray, both he and Gerda had tears glistening in their eyes. The entire family bent their heads down low to pray. Derk led them in a prayer of thanksgiving to their heavenly Father up above.

Three days later, the storm lost most of its fury. Fence posts along the road had disappeared under a blanket of snow. Frozen drifts had piled four feet high around both their homes, lapping over the roofs of the dwellings and outbuildings of the neighbouring farm. The snow smoothed out into an uneven blanket covering huge stretches of land as far as the eye could see.

Gerda watched the mailman stop his car on the side of the road where the snow plough had been. He shovelled snow away from the mailbox to deliver the mail. He left a note for Derk to shovel a pathway to the mailbox or he would not deliver the mail anymore.

Each day, Derk and the boys sank up to their knees in snow as they worked their way to the barns to check the livestock, water the two hundred head of cattle, feed the sows and little piglets, clean the barns, and help Farmer Atkens melt down enough snow for all his cattle to drink each day.

"I'm sure glad Cris told me about the binder-twine to use as guide line to come here and go home with," Derk said to his boys. "We have learned now that once that strong northeast wind whips up, people really do freeze to death in the prairies' gigantic drifts of snow, even when they're only yards away from shelter. I truly believe that now, boys, don't you?"

Derk felt a cold shiver come creeping down his spine. What if any one of them had gotten lost, or frozen to death, in this, their first experience with a frightening snow blizzard?

Gerda, too, was forced to melt snow for water usage. She did not like the taste of snow water, but gradually she got used to this new way of trying to survive.

Temperatures plummeted to forty-five degrees below zero overnight. After three full days, the harsh blizzard laid itself to rest. The air was filled with brilliant ice crystals. The prairies lay glazed and paralysed in the harsh grip of Canadian winter.

Gerda looked out the window, mesmerized at the wonder of it all.

Oh well, there will be warmer days as the seasons roll along, she pondered in her heart. *We best get used to it all.*

16

Farming at Last

Daybreak came at a leisurely pace, slowly rising like a tide of silent colour creating a thin red ribbon along the horizon. The sky was still black, and the stars were out but were fading slowly.

Derk walked around his fully loaded three-ton truck to inspect if the load was tied down securely enough for them to travel six hundred miles west. A bird started singing, its voice piercing the silence of what promised to be a bright sunny day. Derk took a deep breath of the pure early morning air. He paused for a short moment to watch the beauty of nature unfold in the peace and quiet at the beginning of this new adventure.

Derk looked forward to watching the stretched out skies to which there seemed to be no end, and travelling through the newly ploughed fields and the vast stretches of "bald-headed prairies," as people called it.

Gerda and fifteen-year-old Jodi came out the door with two small suitcases. Both of them looked back at the house one more time, as if to say a final goodbye. Gerda then turned to the truck, loaded with items they would need to set up housekeeping on the one hundred sixty acre farm Derk had bought in Rocky Mountain House, a small village in western Alberta with about two thousand residents where both Natives and white people were trying to make a life for themselves together.

"Are you sure this truck is safe to travel such long distance, Derk?" Gerda asked.

It was late April, 1951, three years after the Opden-Dries family immigrated to Canada. By now, they had dwindled down to an eight-member family unit. Hennie, Martin, and Tom had married in the last couple of years.

This Monday morning, the family got up before daylight to get ready for the long trip. Gerda's cousin, Marinus Konynenbelt, had tracked this farm down for Derk. Marinus had promised to come pick up Derk and Gerda's five sons in his fancy big Chevrolet car.

"This is the way to travel, folks!" said twenty-year-old Marcel with a grin on his face from ear to ear. "Let's get going!"

It was near three o'clock in the afternoon when Gerda and Derk arrived at their new place. The sun stood high in the sky. The long driveway up to the house, hidden between tall spruce trees, was little more than a trail through thick and overgrown forest on this densely forested land with forty acres plough-broken and ready for crops. There were thirty-five acres of grassland where two big work horses were grazing peacefully.

Derk started smiling. His mouth curled into a wide grin as he tried manoeuvring the truck through the deeply rutted grooves in the long driveway. *Imagine! Our own place!*

He parked the loaded truck near the front door of a sagging, weather-beaten shack with red and grey shingles on the roof.

Derk, Gerda, and Jodi stepped out of the truck. Derk put both his hands in the pockets of the striped coverall he was wearing. He scanned the land, home, and farm buildings before turning to look at Gerda.

His eyes turned teary. "This will be our home, Gerda, our very own little house on the prairie." He swallowed a time or two. "We've been waiting a long, long time for this moment, Gerda." His face looked as if he were in an emotional turmoil. "A long, long time. This is what I've dreamt of all my life, Gerda, all my life." Derk was visibly emotional.

Jodi watched her dad wipe his eyes with the back of his hand. Ever since Jodi could remember, her dad had been talking about carving a country estate out of dense forest in the wild, wild Western Frontier somewhere in Canada. *Well, here it is.*

Gerda had not even noticed any of the potholes near the front entrance made by heavy rains. Her eyes were glued to the drab little house with faded red-brick siding, two small windows, and a crooked chimney with streaks of black smoke curling up into the sky.

Gerda felt tired and weary. She sighed. So much had changed in their family. The three oldest were married and had found jobs they liked, which left five boys, Jodi, Derk, and herself to start yet another new adventure. They would be farming a quarter section of land and had only forty acres cleared, five cows, four sows, and sixty chickens to work with.

"Come," Derk said, nudging her back to reality. "Let's have a look inside the house."

Marinus Konynenbelt and his brother Hans had been scrubbing and cleaning the house all day. Hans swung open the door with a broad smile face.

"There you are. Great!" Hans took hold of Derk's hand. "I'm so glad you came here to farm." He looked at Gerda. "I… I mean that from the bottom of my heart, Aunt Gerda." He turned suddenly, motioning them to have a look inside.

Gerda followed Hans into the house and almost ran straight into his back when he halted abruptly.

"See!" Hans made a big, round gesture with both his arms. "Nice and clean, Gerda. I couldn't stand you folks coming into a dirty home." Hans looked triumphant.

Gerda closed her eyes and reverently held her hands folded in front of her, as if she had entered paradise prematurely.

The house looked much bigger than the ones they had lived in before. It had three small bedrooms and was well-kept and clean inside.

"Oh, look, Mom!" Jodi started pumping the handle on a pump placed in the sink by the kitchen. The pump squirted fresh clean water into the sink.

"Much better than what we had in Picture Butte." Gerda's voice harboured a tinge of make-believe cheer, her mind already busying itself with plans to make this home cozy, clean, and pleasant to live in.

Her eyes wandered over to the wooden cook stove. It looked clean and fairly new. In the middle of the large room used for both a kitchen and living room there stood a second stove, this one smaller and older, round and fat, near a fireproof wall.

Hans had stoked up the fire in the smaller stove. The kindling crackled as flames rose up the chimney on this unusually cool spring day. Hans piled on a few more logs. The heat from the stove was pleasant, and not too warm.

"This stove heats up to a fourteen-foot radius on cold days," Hans explained, standing up.

Derk smiled mysteriously. "That could come in handy when a blizzard comes to visit, Gerda."

The house inside was otherwise dim and gloomy. There were two kerosene lamps hanging on the ceiling in the big room.

Hmm, a little of bright wallpaper and a coat of fresh paint ought to lend a little cheer to this place, Gerda pondered. *We've been there before.*

Derk came into the living room from one of the bedrooms. "We'll need to put a partition in this room to make us four bedrooms, Gerda." He looked at his wife. His eyes twinkled with sheer delight. "What do you think of this place?"

Gerda was able to master her inner feelings. "This is our own home, Derk. Our very own. That's good enough for me." She paused momentarily. "Yes, good enough for me. You, too?"

They suddenly heard the loud honking of a car. Marinus come walking inside moments later.

A dazzling smile lit his face. "Well, here's the rest of your family, Derk and Gerda."

Derk had worn his favourite red-checked flannelette shirt. With his hands tucked behind braces, a wisp of pitch black hair hung from underneath the dark blue pancake-like hat most farmers wore. He welcomed Marinus. "Thanks for bringing the boys. Sure did find us a mighty nice chunk of land, Marinus. I'm mighty happy with the farm." Derk glanced at Gerda. "I think the house is to Gerda's liking, too."

Gerda smiled. "A little bit of hard work, wallpaper, and paint can make this into a real nice country style home, Marinus. Thanks so much."

Derk turned his head towards a scattered set of farm buildings with jumbled, irregular roofs of red and grey.

"Let's go have a look outside," he said more to the boys than anyone else.

Once outside in the sunshine, Derk shielded his eyes from the glare of the sinking sun. He squinted his eyes. The fine lines around his eyes deepened. He was convinced that none of the buildings had been built with any particular rhyme or reason in mind.

"I am sure neither the house nor any of these farm buildings ever felt the touch of a measuring tape or a bricklayer's cement trowel, Dad," said Sid, the carpenter in the family. "But don't you worry none. We can help you fix them. Sure thing!" Sid puffed up his chest and lifted his chin.

"I'd sure like to start breaking the ground soon so we can put in some grain and seed for haying this fall." Derk felt happy planning with his boys. "Come," he waved, "let me show you a surprise Hans told me about." Derk walked to the back of the barn where Hans had said two horses were under a big tree where the pasture ended.

"Gee willies!" Marcel's voice screeched loud. "Two horses!"

"One of them is saddle broke," Derk explained. "Hans told me."

"Wow! Can I start riding the smaller one right away?"

"No. We best start helping Mom and Jodi with unpacking and finding a place to sleep tonight."

"But Dad, I've been interested in that kind of stuff for a long, long time already. I know lots about horse riding. Let me try, please?"

"Tomorrow, son." Derk tapped him on the right shoulder. "Tomorrow we'll find out just what kind a cowboy stuff you are made of, Marcel." Derk chuckled.

Gerda watched her sons standing besides Derk, grinning from ear to ear.

She cast her gaze towards the little frontier settlement three miles down the road, nestled in a wooded valley. She paused to behold the long ridge of snow-capped Rocky Mountains that stood motionless on the far horizon, still draped in an apron of snow as though they had been painted across the bright blue sky.

"Between the mountains and the town are huge stretches of land and wooded areas where humans are outnumbered by deer, bears, cougars, wild cats, and coyotes," Marinus told Derk and the boys. "It is not fit for colonization yet."

Late that night, Derk and Gerda stood outside in the pale moonlight under the pristine canopy of millions of twinkling stars hovering above.

"How magnificent is God's creation, Gerda?" Derk's voice was filled with deep emotion.

"I just wonder, how come we never noticed the scope of such glorious majestic wonder in nature in the country we left behind?" Gerda pondered with respect and wonder.

Derk sighed. It was not a sigh of fear or worry anymore. "Too busy with worrying, perhaps?"

Both Derk and Gerda remained outside until the clock struck midnight.

That first night, when the coyotes sang in the back of the bushes nearby, like every other night it sent a light shiver down Gerda's spine—more out of amazement than fear.

17

Back at the Western Ranch

It was a pleasant midsummer day with mellow, golden sunshine perfecting a softening touch everywhere. A lulling wind spread about the fragrance of wild flowers blooming in the five-acre meadow in front of the OpdenDries farmhouse. The air was peaceful. The soft flapping eagle's wings overhead could be heard in the serene early morning silence.

Marcel looked into the shiny black stallion's dark eyes. Those eyes held a mysterious look of unknown intent as they stared back. Marcel stared at the massive creature with confidence. His lips pushed forward in the characteristic expression he adopted every time he was about to make a big decision.

The eager young horse started pawing his right front foot up and down, as though wanting to test the uncharted waters between him and his young master. Tension filled the air. It was an indistinct unrest, as if a Western duo was to begin between man and beast.

Marcel felt a spell of horse-busting coming on. “I think I’d like to try one of these horses, Dad,” he said with a manly tone. His eyes twinkled thinking in anticipation of the adventure he was about to undertake.

Derk looked sideways at Marcel, noticed the way he had set his jaw, a sure sign that he Marcel meant what he had just said. “Give it a try, Marcel. But be careful.” Derk’s eyes reflected worry and respect at the same time.

Derk stroked the smaller horse’s nose and spoke softly to him. Marcel was a little nervous, contrary to his brave appearance. He stepped forward and gently stroked the horse’s shiny neck, but only for a moment. The horse tossed its head impatiently and immediately displayed temper.

“I might as well give it a try right this moment,” he said.

With that, Marcel quickly jumped on the horse’s back. The animal seemed to explode into the air, his four feet leaving the ground all at once. Marcel clamped his legs around the horse’s body and hung onto the mane, just as full of defiance as the young horse underneath him. The front feet plummeted down, stabbing the grass pasture again and again.

Marcel bounced forward then back over and over again. The horse appeared to think for a moment, then commenced a dizzying whirl, twisting and turning without any particular pattern.

Although Derk and the four brothers cheered loudly, Gerda was afraid that Marcel would be tossed to the ground violently. She envisioned numerous broken bones in his body.

But the horse decided to use another trick, rearing up on his hind legs, then bouncing forward and back again. Gerda stifled a scream in her throat when the horse decided to race around the pasture with flattened ears and flared nostrils, letting out a high bugle sound each time it flew by Derk and the boys. After three rounds, the horse came to an abrupt halt and lunged forward before galloping around the field again, snorting and neighing as the breeze lifted its mane from its head.

Marcel hung on to the runaway horse's mane, trying to calm it, hoofs clattering and throwing up little tufts of prairie grasses around the ten-acre pasture. The horse came to a sliding stop after rounding the field four times. The overly frisky horse then lifted both his hind legs into the air. Marcel came sailing over the fence and landed with a loud thud near where Derk and the boys were watching.

Derk, Sid, Dick, Johan, and Bert stood in complete silence, staring at Marcel, who had been dumped at their feet. All the smirks were wiped off their faces at once.

"Go get—" But Derk did not have time to finish his sentence. Marcel opened his eyes. He shook his head, rolled over, and pushed himself off the ground with the tips of his fingers.

Marcel rubbed his shoulder. "I'm not going to give up, Dad. It takes more than this to keep a cowboy off a horse. I'll go harness Big Black." Marcel pointed in the direction where the tall horse stood dozing lazily under a tree.

Marcel began harnessing the bigger work horse they called Big Black. He had promised to help Derk plough a field for spring seed planting. It did not take long to harness the horse. Marcel lifted one rein and let it fall on Big Black's hindquarters. Marcel made clacking noises with his tongue, but the horse didn't move. Marcel tried again. The horse looked at him as if ready to fall asleep. Marcel then walked to the head of the horse, yanked hard on the bridle, and tried to pull him along. The horse did not move. Marcel's face showed frustration. His face turned red.

"Here, Johan, hold these reins." Marcel threw the reins towards his younger brother. "Wait till I get back!"

Marcel's harsh tone spelled trouble. He walked into the barn, taking huge steps, and picked up an armful of dried hay. He marched back to the horse, grim-faced, and threw the hay under Big Black's belly.

Marcel clenched his teeth. "There, that ought to make you move, old fella!" He dug into his right shirt pocket and extracted three long-stemmed matches. Marcel bent his knee and struck a match head across the tight blue jeans. The second match lit. He then bent over and threw the lit match on the pile of hay under the horse's belly.

Marcel and the boys watched the flames spread fast. Big Black's spirit came alive suddenly. The horse's round gypsy eyes looked around in an attempt to comprehend what was happening. Snorting loudly, he shook his mane. Then his front paws began clawing in the air. Big Black arched his strong neck and bolted forward, jumped over the fence and disappearing into the woods.

Derk came out of the house, saw Marcel's dejected face, and burst out laughing. He nodded his head towards the thirty acres of land to be ploughed for spring crop seeding. "Come on now, cowboy, seems to me we had better get ourselves a good tractor to do the ploughing." Derk waited until his son looked up at him. Derk smiled understandingly. "I think them horses out here or not very cooperative, are they."

"I suppose we better get a tractor, Dad," Marcel said. "But… but I tell you, Dad, this here cowboy is not giving in that easy, do you hear?"

"I know, son, I know." The two walked towards the house to see if Gerda had the morning coffee ready.

"Marinus has been telling me that there is a cattle auction every Wednesday and a machinery auction every Thursday," Derk said over a cup of coffee. "I think we should all go and have a look at the auction first thing tomorrow morning."

"What about getting a good family car, Dad, so that Mom can go shopping in style for a change?" asked Sid, whose heart was more interested in cars and mechanical things.

Marcel spoke up, his hurt ego already restored. "I've been thinking, Dad. With all that timber on the land, we could easily cut trees and saw them into lumber to add an addition to the back of the house."

"We could cut the smaller trees into fence posts and sell them at the auction this winter, too," Dick piped up, letting his voice be heard. "All we would need is a saw mill and a cross-cut saw, Dad. Let's do it."

Derk frowned, thinking of the future. His eyes wandered towards the rusty old breaking plough standing near the barn. He lifted his gaze towards a large chunk of cleared land, but even that ground still needed to be plough-broken. "I'd sure like to get that field ready for seeding soon. The ground needs one year to rest before we can farm it, so they tell me. Think we can plough break that land, boys?"

Promptly the next morning, Derk and Gerda went to the lawyer's office with Marinus to make a two thousand dollar down payment on the farm. It cost a total of four thousand dollars. The other half had to be paid one year later.

At six o'clock, Derk, Marcel, Dick, Johan and young Bert went to the barn to milk and feed the cows, feed the chickens, and tend to the ten sows with thirty piglets.

Bert came into the house with sparkling eyes and cheeks aglow. He put half a bucket of milk on the kitchen table and strained it into a clean pail which Gerda had made ready for him.

"Dad told me I've got to try churning butter from this," Bert told his mom.

Bert put half the milk in a butter churn Derk had bought at the auction. Gerda put the rest into clean mason jars, then closed them with lids. Bert went ahead and inserted a long wooden dasher into the butter churn and began the steady up-and-down motion that would turn the milk into butter.

Gerda, in her own area of expertise, had been quick to adopt her new role as immigrant wife and mother. Derk's sister Mina had shown her how to shop from Eaton's Catalogue, which Mina jokingly called the "Farmer's Bible."

Derk himself bought a brand new radio for the family and an English language study book, all for seven dollars. Derk wanted to keep up with world news, like he had done all his life. Derk asked Jodi to order the *Prairie Farmer* and the *Weekly Press* newspapers, which cost one dollar per year for each.

"If not for the news, at least we can use the paper to light the stove in the morning, Derk," Gerda chuckled.

18

Sunday

The day looked dark, leaden, and rainy. There was just enough of a breeze to make the air feel cold and damp. The forecast was for rain showers in the morning, sunny in the afternoon. There was a lot of excitement in the little wooden home, more so than there ever had been before in the history of the OpdenDries house.

Gerda stood in front of the little mirror in the bedroom. She felt happy and light-hearted this morning, Sunday, a day of rest. Ever since Derk had shown her their family car, their first ever, Gerda's usually humble walk in life had been given a big enough boost to lift her ego plumb across the borderline of meekness into vain glory.

It was Sunday, the end of April 1951.

Outfitting herself for the Sunday church service in Rocky Mountain House, Gerda looked back over the week gone by. The first week had passed so quickly. On their first day in the new home, she and Jodi had tried to organize the place to make it look like a cozy, country style home. There still was a lot more work to be done, however. Rooms needed to be painted and wallpapered.

"But all good things come in due time, slow but sure," Gerda reminded everyone more than once.

Derk and the boys went to a cattle auction on Wednesday, where Derk bought more cows, sows, and chickens. At a machinery sale the next day, Derk bought a John Deere tractor, a washing machine with a gas motor, two large washtubs, and a 1936 Model-A Ford car for family use.

Gerda started humming softly. She put on her black Sunday hat and pulled down the rim towards the right a little, just enough for the hat to rest comfortably on her right ear while exposing her left ear a quarter of an inch. Gerda walked over to the closet and took a big black leather purse off a spike inside. She walked into the kitchen with her purse freely dangling on her left arm.

Derk, Jodi, and the five boys were waiting, dressed in their Sunday best.

"Best get going, Gerda," Derk spoke, glancing at the clock. "Church starts at ten o'clock."

Gerda followed them outside. It was raining hard. She paused momentarily and looked at the car eight feet away from her.

It isn't worth digging my umbrella out of my skirt pocket, she thought. On her way to the car, she pushed back her hat to prevent raindrops from falling on her face.

Gerda was not quite sure if it was better to protect her face from the rain with the rim of her hat tilted forward or to let the hat slope backwards and risk having raindrops trickle down the back of her neck. *At least the car will be dry inside,* she whispered to herself.

It was so wonderful now that they had their own car to go to church with. The boys were not forced to sit in the back of the three-ton truck any longer! Gerda sighed, but with pleasure.

The Model-A was nice and clean inside. Jodi had spent all afternoon the day before washing it. Derk held open the door so that Gerda and Jodi could hop into the back seat with three of the boys. It was cramped, but it would have to do. The two oldest boys sat up front with Derk.

Johan noticed that the rusty door hinges made a creaking sound. "We'll need to oil them hinges tomorrow," he mumbled loudly.

"The mechanical mind at work once more," Derk said with a smile.

Gerda encountered trouble working her way into the back seat. The edge of the wide ruffled skirt she wore hooked behind a screw sticking out of the doorframe. She frowned. Derk bent over to unhook her skirt. Gerda puffed, seated herself, and took a small umbrella out of the large skirt pocket. She positioned it on top of her lap, then readjusted her hat once more.

Derk was the last one to jump in the car out of the pouring rain. He gave the car keys to Marcel. "Here, you been driving in Rocky Mountain House all week already. You drive us to church, please."

Marcel looked full of surprise. "Me? In our family car?"

"Why sure! I'm mighty proud to be sitting beside my oldest farm boy going to church, Marcel." It sounded like a little bit of emotion was creeping into Derk's voice.

Marcel looked robust and valiant manoeuvring the narrow-wheeled car as it crawled its way through the early spring mud puddles brought on by the heavy overnight rainfall. The rain continued to hurl a drumming cascade of water against the front window. The tires, worn through to the canvas on all four wheels, made driving tricky.

Derk noticed a few beads of sweat forming on Marcel's brow. The tracks in the muddy were so deep that Marcel had a hard time keeping the car out of the ditches.

"We'll be getting new tires before winter comes, Marcel," Derk encouraged.

Once Marcel hit the main road, he got the feel of the car and put the pedal to the metal in short order. The car rattled along. Gerda felt proud and happy with this, their very own car. It was like a haven in an uncharitable world of rain and mud.

Gerda suddenly felt a driving wind come swirling around her stocking feet. The rain that had gathered in the dips and valleys of the canvas rooftop now began dripping through. A small pool of water was gathering on her lap.

Derk also noticed muddy water coming inside the car through gaps in the floorboards. "Stop! Marcel!"

Marcel stepped on the brakes and parked the car near a ditch.

Gerda calmly got her umbrella and clicked the button on the umbrella handle. It exploded into a mushrooming parachute. She held the umbrella over the back seat passengers. "This ought to keep us dry!" she said with a chuckle. There was a twinkle in her eyes. Somehow, Gerda could not feel depressed on this day.

"You want me to drive a ways, son?" Derk asked Marcel.

"No, Dad. I'll be just fine. Just fine."

The car continued to hobble along over the narrow, bumpy road. The engine began to make woeful grinding noises until they reached the Rocky Mountain House Community Hall, where church services were held twice every Sunday.

The small, dark and dreary building had paint blistering on the outside walls. It had four small windows on the south side facing the road.

Marcel let his family out near the door of the church hall. Derk got out and walked to the other side. He opened the door to help Gerda and the rest of the family out of the car.

Gerda pushed the button on her umbrella once again. It mushroomed open. She hovered the umbrella over Jodi, and as far as she could reach over Derk and the boys to protect them from the pouring rain that came down in waves.

She followed Derk in her usual graceful manner through the front door entrance of the building. A look of elegance surrounded her and her tidy looking family. Entering the front porch, she blinked in the fairly large, dark surroundings.

The community hall was used for all sorts of occasions during the week. Inside, it showed that someone had cared enough to set up two rows of twelve benches with an aisle running down the middle and up to the front. About fifty people were sitting on the rows of wood-slatted benches.

A small stage had a piano in the right hand corner. There was a small homemade pulpit for the preacher to give his sermon to the faithful followers of Christianity.

Gerda followed Derk to the fifth bench from the front. Even though Gerda had never seen anyone here before, her interest in people was seemingly endless. She let her habitually friendly smile reach her eyes, and said a soft "Hello" to the other worshippers she passed along the way.

Once seated, Gerda held up her skirt stiffly so it would not brush against the dusty wooden floor. She sat clear-eyed beside Derk, holding her hands reverently on her lap. She felt a cheerful serenity deep down inside. Her interest turned reflective as she smiled peacefully, as if all was at ease with her.

The church pastor, a tall man in his fifties whose hair was just beginning to be touched by grey, entered from a little room next to the pot-bellied wood stove in the front. His eyes were blue and he looked impressive, dressed in a black suit, white shirt, matching tie, and black shoes.

The pastor stopped to overlook the crowd. His bright eyes held a desperate light as they wandered around the room. His features seemed to soften, then the unfailingly courteous man, came walking over towards Derk and Gerda. He shook their hands with a certain gentleness that showed in his mannerisms.

Derk and the pastor eyed each other for a slight moment. His kind, blue eyes, demonstrating his core friendliness, made Derk wish he were a friendlier person himself.

A base rumble came from the pastor's throat. "We wish to welcome you to our congregation. We certainly hope each of you will enjoy your stay with us here today." He turned to look at Jodi and her five brothers seated beside Gerda. The pastor asked Derk to come with him. At the end of the hall, the pastor took time to give Derk a small glimpse into his good-natured character. He turned to look at Derk, a smile sliding across his face. "I wonder, Mr. OpdenDries, could there be a piano player amongst any one of your children, perhaps?"

"Yes, indeed," said Derk. "Marcel loves playing all sorts of music. I'm sure he will lead the congregational singing, Pastor." Derk nodded in Marcel's direction. "Marcel, the pastor asked if you would play the piano for the singing today. Would you?"

"Oh, sure. No problem, Dad. Where do I go?" A fearless look spread across his face. Marcel got up, puffed out his chest, and lifted his chin so as to look just a little taller. He rolled his shoulders, and with a wave of the hand to his parents he went up on stage and sat behind the piano. He started paging through the praise songbook.

Derk slipped his calloused hand into Gerda's left hand. He gently squeezed her hand, a silent signal of deep understanding between the two.

The six-foot-two, broad-shouldered pastor walked over to the homemade pulpit in the middle of the room. All the people sat down. Silence filled the room. The pastor's big twinkling eyes quietly observed the audience.

"Good morning to you all," he announced in a deep, low voice. "This morning we are happy to have with us a young piano player, Marcel OpdenDries." The pastor nodded in Marcel's direction. "Marcel has graciously agreed to play the piano for the congregational singing this Sunday."

The pastor's face radiated happiness.

Marcel stood up and bowed. He quietly closed the curtains up on the stage so that no one could see him play the piano. He felt better playing with the curtains closed.

Jodi figured the preacher must be close to sixty years old. He was a little worn and tired looking, but once he got up to deliver his sermon there was fire in his voice. His face was glowing.

Midway through the sermon, Gerda shifted back a little to what she hoped would be a more comfortable position on the slatted seats. A few of the slats dug into her skin uncomfortably.

Jodi glanced sideways. She bent forward a tiny bit and saw Derk and Gerda caught up in the sermon. Gerda's face was radiant and full of contentment. When the minister closed his Bible and said a loud "Amen!" Derk nodded a solemn agreement with the words the preacher had spoken.

The Lord sure does not need a hearing aid to hear this pastor preach, Jodi chuckled.

The pastor took a white handkerchief out of his jacket pocket and wiped the sweat off his brow. "Come, let us sing, number 350 in the hymnbook, 'Praise God from Whom All Blessings Flow.'" The congregation rose to their feet. Marcel did not start to play the piano.

"Uh-oh!" The pastor looked mildly amused. "Let us sing together," he repeated with a loud voice. There still was no reaction from behind the curtain.

The pastor slowly walked towards the closed curtain on the stage and shoved them aside. A smile slid across his face. Marcel lay with outstretched legs, peacefully snoring.

Gerda threw back her head and blushed. Derk let a merry laugh curl round his lips.

"Marcel, wake up. I think it's time to go home!" said the pastor.

"Uh-oh, did I miss something?" Marcel blurted out.

"Just a little, son, just a little." There was deep understanding in the preacher's voice. "Shall we sing number 350 in your hymnbook, please?"

Bewildered, Marcel started fiercely attacking the innocent bone-white keyboard in front of him. He hammered out the tune with firm hands, loud and clear.

After the service, everyone departed in small groups and gathered outside the building under a veranda.

Derk, Gerda, and the rest of the family made quick friendships.

That evening, the weather turned cool and pleasant. Derk and Gerda sat by a homemade picnic table. They had learned to enjoy admiring the dazzling beauty of nature in the skies late at night. Derk put both his elbows on the table and rested his face in the cup of his hands. He turned his face towards the sky and start counting the millions of twinkling stars hovering over the earth in the magnificent canopy.

He suddenly turned to look at Gerda beside him. In deep thought, he asked, "Do you feel sorry we ever left Holland, Gerda?" Derk watched her eyes in the bright moonlight.

Gerda kept watching the glowing full moon up above, hovering in the sky like a gigantic ball in the sparkling firmament. She remained quiet, but only for a little while. When Derk put his arms around her, she felt grateful for that comfort.

She swallowed a big lump in her throat. "No, Derk, not anymore. I have come to understand that our heavenly Father up above has been weaving a colourful tapestry all along in the lives of our family throughout the war years, in our new homeland, and through all the days of our lives." Gerda spoke with tried and tested understanding. She looked up towards Derk beside her. "I will thank Him for that grace and mercy, Derk, always." Her broad smile beamed inner peace.

Derk knew she told the truth. She always did.

CPSIA information can be obtained at www.ICGtesting.com
226285LV00004B/1/P

9 781770 692664